THE WATCHER

BELLA JEWEL

St. Martin's Paperbacks

This is a work of fiction. All of the characters, organizations, and events portrayed in this novel are either products of the author's imagination or are used fictitiously.

THE WATCHER

Copyright © 2017 by Bella Jewel.

Excerpt from *Blind Date* copyright © 2017 by Bella Jewel.

For information address St. Martin's Press, 175 Fifth Avenue, New York, NY 10010.

ISBN: 978-1-250-10838-8

Our books may be purchased in bulk for promotional, educational, or business use. Please contact your local bookseller or the Macmillan Corporate and Premium Sales Department at 1-800-221-7945, ext. 5442, or by e-mail at MacmillanSpecialMarkets@macmillan.com.

Printed in the United States of America

St. Martin's Paperbacks edition / June 2017

St. Martin's Paperbacks are published by St. Martin's Press, 175 Fifth Avenue, New York, NY 10010.

10 9 8 7 6 5 4 3 2 1

Acclaim for the novels of Bella Jewel

"You can't go wrong with a Bella Jewel book."
—*Lustful Literature*

"The story was fresh, unique, sexy, and loaded with mystery and intrigue. The dynamic characters came to life and jumped off the pages. Enthralling!"
—*Smut Book Junkie*

"A hot-as-hell ride . . . I expect nothing less from Bella." —*A Hopeless Romantic's Booklandia*

"An entertaining, hot read that will keep you on your toes." —*Rochelle's Reviews*

"A sexy, dramatic suspense that I didn't want to put down!" —*Harlequin Junkies*

"Fast-paced, action-packed, steamy story. Definitely grab it if you like strong, kick-butt heroines, an alpha hero who wants to care for her, and lots of action and romance!" —*Crystal's Many Reviewers*

"Bella Jewel knows how to write herself a female lead and bring us all with her for the ride."
—*Readful Things Blog*

"Sexy, irresistible, this story was addicting! I read it all in one sitting and I couldn't get enough."
—*The Novel Tease*

"Brazen and a bit of a thrill, it just works on all cylinders." —*Smexy Books*

Also by Bella Jewel

72 HOURS

PROLOGUE

Breathe in. Breathe out.

Breathe in. Breathe out.

"Marlie, I know you're in here."

A deranged singsong voice fills the overly quiet space, making my skin prickle. I think it's the tone that makes it feel worse—that chipper, no-regrets tone that tells you with one simple word just how crazy he is. It tells you the limits he'll go to, to achieve exactly what he wants. Death. Slow and painful. Tortured.

Breathe.

Just breathe.

Humorless laughter rings out. "You don't *actually* think you can escape me, do you?"

Cold, clammy sweat runs down my forehead and I'm shaking all over as I scoot further back into the closet. Why did I pick a closet? I don't understand what possessed me to do something so stupid. My one chance at freedom, and I lock myself in a place I can't escape from. I wasn't thinking. I was just running, and all my instincts told me to hide. That's what I did. It wasn't until after I got in here that I realized what a stupid mistake that was, and now I'm trapped. It's too late to try to get out.

Another shiver travels through my body as I peer into the light coming through the tiny crack in the door. Maybe I can swing it open and slam it in his face. That might buy me a few minutes. But I can't see well enough to know the exact moment he might be close enough to do that. I'm relying on the lighting, but that's flickering and dull at best.

"I know you're in here, you're not smart enough to outrun me. We can do this the easy way, or the hard way. If you want me to kill you slowly, stay hidden. If you want it to be quick, come on out. Either way, you will die, Marlie. It's part of the plan. You understand that, right?"

Sick.

He's speaking to me as if I'm no more than an employee, or a naughty child. Like it's completely normal to stand there and discuss my death. As if having options will make it feel any better.

I clench my eyes shut, trying to force back the burning bile rising up in my throat. I can't be sick now; if I'm sick it'll take away my focus and he'll get hold of me for sure. And I know what he'll do. First, he'll break my knees, because that's what he does. I read all about him. Everyone did. I know exactly who has me. After he's broken my knees, he'll start peeling my skin. . . . Bile burns my throat and I inwardly scream, praying this is just a horrible, sick dream.

But I know it's not.

"Oh Marlie Marlie Marlie, why do you have to make things so hard on yourself? It's as if you want to die a slow and painful death. Which is fine by me, but surely you're a little smarter than that."

A tiny, broken cry leaves my throat and I clench my eyes shut, fists balled, wondering why I didn't get a weapon. Why didn't I go for the front door? Honestly, what the hell was I thinking running in here? Of course he'd find me, of course he'd know where I'd go. He's done this thirteen times before. Successfully.

Not one girl has escaped.

The closet door swings open and I'm faced with cold, deadly blue eyes and a crooked smile. You would probably pass him on the street and not once suspect that he's capable of this. Hell, I had no clue. He had dropped his briefcase and I'd leaned down to help him pick it up, then bam, he'd held a rag over my nose and before I knew it I was bound and lying in the back of a white van. All alone and terrified. He made it seem so simple.

All because I was being a good person.

Life is a bitch like that.

Deranged eyes pin mine, and he laughs hysterically as he looks down at my pitiful attempt at me. "There you are. You know, a few of the girls have tried to escape me. One nearly succeeded. I punished her severely—her death was the slowest."

I try to scurry backwards, only to hit the wall with a thump. The breath is ripped out of my lungs and all my instincts beg me to scream for help, but I know as well as he does that there's no help coming.

There never is in this situation, is there?

He swings the bat, and it hits my kneecaps.

I drop to the ground, hands hitting the old, faded carpet. I roll to my back, screaming in pain. He hits me again, this time the bat connecting with my shins.

He keeps going, driving the bat down over my legs. I can hear my own bones breaking, but I can do nothing to fight him off.

All I can do is lie there screaming, and wishing for death.

I spit blood on the floor as I drag my broken, pathetic body towards the kitchen counter. I don't even know how I'm still alive. He's shattered my knees, or the bones around them, or my whole legs, I don't know. All I know is I want to die, but I can't. I won't. Somehow, I'm here, dragging my body towards the counter at a rapid pace, sweat rolling down my face, my body screaming at me to just stop.

I can't.

I screwed up my escape once. It won't happen again.

I reach the counter and haul myself up, my bruised hands somehow managing to grip tight enough for me to get to my feet. I scream in pain, but I'm no longer trying to be quiet. I don't even know how I got away from him. He drugged me, but as if my prayers had been answered, I apparently woke earlier than planned and pretended I was asleep as he moved around me.

He unbound me and began to move me, probably to prepare for my gruesome end, but I managed to take him by surprise. I raised my shattered knee and hit him so hard in the groin he stumbled backwards. It was, without a doubt, the worst pain I've ever felt in my life. I managed to drag myself off the bed and reached for the lamp beside it. Before he could get up, I slammed it into his head, knocking him out.

Then I got the hell out of there. It's amazing what the human body can do when it has to. Somehow I pull my broken and damaged body out of the room, even though the pain is excruciating.

It's only been a matter of minutes, but it feels like hours. I don't feel like I'm moving quickly enough. He's coming for me. Once he came to from his moment of blackness, I heard him get up. Seconds. It's all I have. I reach for the kitchen knives and pull the first one out. I've never thought about killing another person, but right now I'm more than willing to take another life for the sake of my own.

"I'll peel your skin from your body!" he roars

as he stumbles out. "Then I'll stuff it down your throat until you gag on your own flesh."

I hold the knife close and let my body lower to the ground, pulling myself closer to the counter so I'm protected. I have one chance only. It's not much, but it's all I have. My fingers tremble around the cold steel of the handle, as I press it to my chest and swallow the bile in my throat over and over, praying it stays down.

Just for one more minute.

A sharp pain radiates through my skull, taking me off guard, and I realize he's come from above me. He takes handfuls of my hair, his large body lying over the top of the counter as he reaches down, trying to haul me up. I scream as chunks of it dislodge from my scalp and, because of the pain, the knife in my hand skitters to the floor.

"I'll rip your fucking skin from your body, inch by fucking inch."

He tugs again, and through my blurred vision I desperately reach for the knife. I scream in agony as he tugs again and again, and finally I get hold of it, curling my bloodied fingers around its handle. I look up, and through the blood running down my face and over my eyes I take one last look at the man I know will forever haunt my dreams. But I do what I have to do, no matter what kinds of scars will be left behind.

I drive the knife upwards.

ONE

Chirp chirp.

Groaning, I throw my hand over my face. Morning already? Another day? *Really*. It seems I only went to bed five minutes ago, how could it possibly be time to wake up? The dramatic singing of the birds outside indicate that it is, in fact, morning, and that means I've made it to see the light of another day. Another lonely, dragging day of misery.

Okay, that's slightly dramatic, but what can I say? It's my life now.

More loud chirping makes me throw my arm from my face and slap it down on the bed beside me. "All right, I'm up," I grumble, attempting to sit.

My body aches and my head is pounding. It seems I wake up this way more often than not these days. The doctor tells me it's all in my head, that there is nothing physically wrong with me anymore. He didn't get his entire body beaten with a bat, so what the hell would he know? I feel it every time I move. My legs mostly. An ache that seems like it'll never leave, a soreness in my muscles that I'm constantly trying to stretch out.

I shove myself up to a sitting position, and stare out the window. I see nothing but trees. Just a vast expanse of skinny, yet lush, trees. There's nowhere else I'd rather be, and that's the honest truth. I bought this tiny, one-bedroom cabin just outside of Colorado Springs for a bargain three years ago. The owner gave me a great deal because he had an emergency with his family and needed to sell it urgently. It was a dream come true for me.

I left my home in Denver just before that, around the time I went from being a nobody to a famous serial killer survivor. I don't say this lightly. Fame didn't come as a relief; it came as my own personal hell. I was suffering serious mental instability, but my mother figured, *Hey, why not put my daughter in the spotlight by writing a novel about her horrible ordeal with a deranged psychopath?* I'll never forget the hours she sat, talking to reporters, the police, and me about what happened. She managed to piece together enough information to make a bestseller.

Seemed like a solid plan.

The book took off, became massive overnight. So did I.

Then came the time I couldn't walk down the street without being noticed by someone. If it wasn't insane requests for autographs—*Really, who does that?*—it was people staring at me like I was a zoo animal. They were either too afraid to talk to me, scared no doubt that I might have a giant breakdown, or wanted to ask me a million non-sensical questions about my kidnapping. As if they were casually discussing a movie and not a human life.

I played along for a while, for the sake of my family—mostly for my widowed mother, who was smiling for the first time since my father died only a year before my kidnapping. But later, I struggled with knowing that her happiness came from ex-ploiting my pain. After all, her daughter nearly lost her life, but then, she was making millions from my story, so what the hell, right?

I was suddenly a survivor. The girl who got away. The brave one. The one who got a second chance at life.

I didn't want any of that.

I don't know why I didn't pack up and run ear-lier, but the truth is I didn't even know my name most days. Intense therapy and people screaming for my story on the street made my already trau-matized mind shut down. I lived most days like a zombie, moving through life purely because I had to, not because I wanted to. Instead of supporting me, my mother made my ordeal about her. Resent-ment lives deep in my chest daily because of that.

Because she wasn't there for me when she needed to be. Because she didn't help me when I was suffering. Because she didn't comfort me when I'd wake up screaming from the nightmares.

The god-awful nightmares.

Even now, I see his face every time I close my eyes. My therapist assures me it won't be this way forever. I think she's wrong. I think it'll be this way for the rest of my life. I just don't see how talking to someone about it is going to take away the fact that he's in my head, and I'm damned sure he'll never leave.

But I'm surviving, now that I'm out here, on my own; I'm making it through. Some days I don't know how, but I think the solitude helps. No reporters. No family members. No walking down the street with judgment. No fear. It's just me. I feel safe, which is something I haven't felt in such a long time.

I throw myself out of bed and my knees protest angrily, but I push on. I don't need any more reminders about what he did. My knees like to keep my mind in the past. Part of the reminder is my fault, I guess. After all, I picked the worst job there is for weak knees—waitressing. In my defense, living this far out of Denver, it was really the only option for me.

My boss is understanding.

Mostly.

Except for days like today, when I sleep in.

I don't need to work. In fact, I probably won't

need to work for the rest of my life, but I refuse to touch money that has come from a monster and the story he created for me. I gave most of it to my mom, but in my own account there's a good few million that I don't touch. It just keeps growing and growing as the book continues to sell. I don't want it. I don't think I'll *ever* want it.

I half walk, half flail, to my closet and pull out my work clothes, which consist of a short black miniskirt and a tight tank top. The diner is a little run-down, so my boss insists on making it more attractive by making *us* look more attractive. I wear leggings under my skirt, because the scarring on my knees is far too hideous. My boss is fine with it. I think he knew he didn't really get a choice.

Without time for a shower, I drop my nightie and pull the clothes on, before throwing my hair up into a ponytail and jerking on some shoes. There, I'm ready. I groan my way out into the tiny kitchen and head straight to my coffee machine, praying I remembered to set it for this morning.

When it roars to life, I sigh happily.

Thank the heavens.

I take my coffee and pour it into my travel mug. And then I grab my keys and rush out the door. I really need to set an alarm, but that would mean committing to something, and this year I've promised myself I'll just let life take me where it wishes. Yeah right, who am I kidding? I just find comfort in my bed, and most nights it takes me so long to fall asleep that when I finally do, I hang on to it. That usually lasts well into the morning.

I get into the small, beat-up truck my boss gave me when he decided he was far too impatient to fix it, and I had a friend of mine sort it out for me. He has a crush on me, or he did, and so he did it for free. Plus, he was one of those guys that would do anything for another person. For a time, I felt like people did things for me only because they felt sorry for me, but it turns out, some people just liked helping. Sometimes people have no idea who I am and I can have normal conversations without judgment, intrusive questions, or those looks people give when they feel sorry for you.

I don't go anywhere else. I haven't been home to Denver to see my mother or sister, Kaitlyn, for the last few years. They visit me, but the idea of going back into that city, and facing people, is just too much to handle. It just reminds me of everything that went wrong in my life. I'm close enough that they can easily access me when they need to, but far enough that I no longer feel the heavy burden of my past.

I know this affects Kaitlyn.

She suffered when I was taken. She was terrified and thought she'd never see me again. I can't imagine what it was like for her. I'm all she has. We were always super close, especially after our dad died and Mom went off the rails. Kaity and I were all we had and we grew to rely on each other.

My mother put her whole focus on me and the

media surrounding me after I was taken, and suddenly Kaitlyn didn't matter anymore. It bothered Kaitlyn, and lately that's showing. The last time mother dearest called, she told me Kaitlyn was seeing a new man, and he was into drugs and all sorts of terrible things.

When I called Kaity, she assured me Mom was losing her mind and that everything was fine.

I wasn't sure I believed her, so I asked our mutual friend Hannah to keep an eye on her for me. Kaity and I met Hannah not long after I returned from my horror. She befriended Kaity at a yoga class, and when Kaity brought her over, she was so kind to me. No judgment. A breath of fresh air. So unlike the other people in my life. We all became great friends. She's been reporting back to me for a few weeks now, letting me know that things aren't as good as Kaity is saying. I trust Hannah.

I just hope Kaitlyn is letting her in, because I'm becoming concerned.

My sister is the only thing I have left.

TWO

"Order up!"

Paul, my boss, slides some plates onto the stainless steel counter and slaps the bell over and over, glaring at me with those deep-brown eyes. He really is a good man at heart, but he works his staff hard. He expects dedication from them and mostly, he gets it. Except from me. But he's learned to tolerate my ups and downs. Some days—*most days*—I'm a fierce worker. But others, like today, I struggle.

Paul was kind to me when I came to town and asked him for a job. He'd seen my face on the news, and he knew what I'd been through. He gave me the job without hesitation. He never asked questions. He didn't judge and he didn't push. Paul has a kind heart, the type that will always give without question. I'll be forever grateful to him for that.

"I can hear you dude, cool it." I grin and he glares at me, but I don't miss the way his lips twitch.

"I just thought I'd wake you up. You look like you didn't sleep last night, Lee."

Paul is the only person who calls me Lee and honestly, I don't mind. I hate the name Marlie. I always said it reminds me of a dog, and what would you know, there was even a movie about a dog called Marley. Honestly. What are the odds?

I give him a weak smile. "I didn't, but I can still bring in the tips like there's no tomorrow. Even on a bad day."

He finally cracks and winks at me. "I have no doubt. Take a break after you take these plates out; you've been working for six straight hours."

I glance down at my watch. Holy crap, I have.

Yeesh. No wonder why my legs have been killing me.

"No problem."

I take the plates and deliver them to the intended table, smiling politely at the customers, and then go to take my break. I grab my phone, and a croissant out of the warmer, and head out back to the small rickety chair that all Paul's staff use to smoke, eat, and do other things on. I don't even want to know what those other things are, but I hear this chair has stories.

I take a bite of the buttery croissant and stare

down at my phone. Seven missed calls. Four from Hannah, three from my mother. My mother only ever calls when she wants to "borrow" more money. Even though she can just take it when she wants it, she thinks she's doing a good thing by getting my permission. She called for money just two days ago, so it's unusual to see another call from her this soon after. But the ones from Hannah are concerning. I quickly check for texts but there are only some alerting me to voicemail.

Skipping them, I call Hannah right away.

"Marlie, I'm so sorry," she says breathlessly into the phone. "I know you're at work and I wouldn't have called unless it was important."

She seems panicked. My heart starts to pound.

"Hannah, is everything okay?"

"Look, you know I wouldn't worry you over nothing, but Kaitlyn is missing."

My blood runs cold. "What do you mean she's missing?"

"I mean she's just gone. I told you I've been keeping an eye on her. You knew she's been going out with that Chris guy, and I recently learned she started doing drugs. I was going to tell you, but she begged me not to, said it was only a one-time thing. I hadn't heard from her since yesterday so I went over today and . . ."

"And what?" I ask, my throat so tight it burns.

"And her place was trashed. Things were thrown around everywhere, but she's not there. It's been eighteen hours now, and I can't find her."

No.

Oh God.

A familiar pang of fear grips my chest. An automatic paranoia. My brain goes to the worst possible situation and it clings on.

"Have you called the police?"

"I have, and I called your mom, but Marlie, you need to come home."

My mind spins. Home. *Home.* No, I can't go home. I don't want to go home. Goddammit. I don't want to return to that place, but for Kaitlyn . . . dammit . . . I have to.

"I just know something is wrong," Hannah continues. "She's been with this horrible man and his awful friends. Something bad is happening; you need to be here, your mother is a mess."

"Okay," I say in a tiny, shaky voice. "Okay Hannah, just give me today to get the time off."

"I'll be here waiting, call me when you get in. It'll be okay, Marlie."

"Will it?" I whisper.

"I'm sure it will, just come quickly."

"Okay. Bye," I whisper to no one, because she's already gone.

Even though I know she's not lying to me, I still dial my sister's number. It rings and rings. My chest gets even tighter, and I try again. Again nothing. Kaity always answers or texts to let me know she can't talk. It's our thing. Panic turns to real fear as I try to come up with a reasonable explanation in my mind. Maybe she just needs some time away. Maybe she lost her phone. Maybe she's with friends. Maybe she's just busy. I go over all these scenarios, but I can feel it deep in my gut.

She's not okay.

I turn my dry eyes, eyes that haven't cried for three years, to the line of thick trees and beg my heart to stop pounding.

But mostly, I beg for Kaitlyn to return safely before I have to go back there. If I go back there, all the monsters I've put to bed will rise up once more. All the memories, all the nightmares, all the familiar fear and desperation, they'll all come back. I'll be forced to remember the horrible months that followed my escape. I'll have to relive the nightmare I've tried so hard to forget.

I don't want to go back there.

THREE

The sun is blaring down through my windshield as I round the corner to my mother's mansion. There are police cars lined up outside, and the moment my eyes fall on them, my stomach drops. It's been thirty-six hours. Kaitlyn is officially missing.

My sister. The only one in my family who's ever truly cared. The only person who understands what I went through. Now I don't know where she is or what she's going through.

I pull my truck up onto the curb and stare at the massive, three-story home my mother had built after my book took off. I have been in there once and haven't been back since—just looking at it reminds me that it's built from my horror. How can it even feel like a home, considering what it's based on? A shiver ripples through my body and I rub my sweaty palms over my jeans. I glance into the rearview mirror and take note of how awful I look. My honey-colored hair is thrown up in a messy ponytail and my steel-grey eyes seem vacant—better yet, they match the dark rings under them. I look like shit.

I swallow and then throw open the door and walk with shaky legs up to the front of my mother's house. I don't knock, I just walk in. Four police officers are sitting at her large round dining table. One of them has his hand on her back, rubbing gently as he tries to talk to her. Her blonde hair is falling onto the glass tabletop in a perfect mess, and her shoulders are shaking.

I clear my throat.

Five sets of eyes turn to me.

I recognize two of them. Officer Black and Officer Haynes. They were there when I was rescued. I liked Black, but Haynes was an insensitive prick. If I know my mother, she would have requested them specifically on this case. There are hundreds of officers in Denver, but she chose to get these two. They were aware of our family's fame and would be sure to give her the celebrity treatment. Black scoots his chair back, his blue eyes wide as he strides over to me, a weary smile on his face. "I never thought I'd see the day. Marlie, how are you?"

He reaches me and extends his arms for a hug that I stiffly return. Ever since my kidnapping, physical contact bothers me. I'll tolerate it when I have to, but I'd prefer *not* to have to. He pats my back and then releases me, smiling down. His hair, which was dark last time I saw him, is slowly going gray on the sides. It suits him, makes him look more sophisticated.

"Marlie!"

My mother's screeching makes me spin around. She stands and darts towards me, arms open. Without warning, she thrusts herself against me, throwing her arms around my neck. I pat her on the back like she has an illness, and stiffly stand and wait for her to let me go. When she does, she's crying. Big fat tears roll down her cheeks.

"I don't know where she is. Oh, Marlie."

"It'll be okay, Mom," I say in a monotone voice, before turning to Black. "What's being done?"

He sighs and waves a hand towards the chairs. I go towards one, glaring at Haynes as I do. He glares right back. Prick. I sit down. Black and Mom join the table again.

"As I was just saying to your mother, Kaitlyn has been spending time with some less than honorable people. We arrested one of them for dealing hard drugs, and I heard from an informant just last week that she's been seen more and more with this group."

"How will this help us find her?" I ask. He sighs and runs his hands through his hair, looking tired and worn. "Marlie, at this stage there's nothing to indicate anything horrible has happened to Kaitlyn.

Her boyfriend Chris left town, so there's a good chance she's just gone with him, in which case we have no legal right to stop her."

"She wouldn't do that," I protest. "She wouldn't just get up and leave without telling anyone."

"She's been acting out lately," Mom cries. "You don't understand, Marlie. She's in a bad place."

"Maybe she is," I snap. "But surely you can't just assume that she decided to leave. Her apartment was trashed."

"And it doesn't look like anything was stolen," Black says gently. "Not even cash. My guess is it was someone looking for drugs. There was no sign of a struggle. We're looking into this, but unfortunately it doesn't take priority as there's a high chance that Kaitlyn has chosen to leave. While the apartment was in bad shape, it wasn't overly suspicious. These things happen all the time."

"You don't know what's happened with her, though," I yell, frustrated. "She's not answering her phone, and she *always* answers me. She might not even *be* with this Chris man, did you consider that? What if someone else got her? What if—"

"Marlie," Black says, placing his hand on my shoulder and giving me a soft look that makes me want to slap his hand away. "I don't believe Kaitlyn has been taken. I believe she's with Chris, but we're still investigating to be sure."

"How long will that take?" I ask. "If someone has her, moving fast can save her life."

He looks unconcerned. "It's hard to say."

"Are you looking for Chris in the meantime?"

"We're trying, but it's proving to be harder than we first thought. He doesn't run with the best crowd, and his friends haven't exactly been forthcoming with the police."

"That's my sister!" I yell, hands trembling. "You need to try harder."

"Yes, I know you're worried, and I promise you I'll do everything I can."

"But there's no guarantee, right?"

He looks sad. "Sorry, no. Troubled individuals run away all time and we do what we can. But unless we have reason to believe she's in danger, we are unable to progress further than a basic search."

"She didn't run away," I whisper. "I feel it in my gut. And what about her phone being disconnected? When I first called a few days ago, it was still ringing. Why has it stopped now?"

"If she doesn't want to be found, Marlie, then she won't be. A disconnected phone isn't necessarily a concern—it's a simple enough thing to do."

"Something isn't right, Black."

His eyes grow soft. "We're looking into it. I will do all I can. I promise you that."

That's just not enough.

I wander aimlessly through Mom's house after the officers leave. It's massive, filled with the finest furniture, yet it feels so damned empty. There is not a single bit of warmth to be found anywhere. It's worse than a show home. It's a show home built on a foundation of darkness. I shiver and rub my hands up and down my arms when I hear a throat clear behind me. I spin around and exhale with relief and happiness to see Hannah standing in the hall.

"Hannah!" I smile weakly, stepping towards my friend. She extends her arms for me and I go into them, letting her hug me. Outside of Kaity, she's the only person I can handle touching me, and even then, it's only for a short period of time.

"How are you?" she asks.

"I'm fine. The police left a while ago."

She steps back and studies me. She has the prettiest blue eyes, and with her dark hair, it makes quite a combination. "What did they say?"

I sigh. "That she has been getting into trouble lately, and they think that she's left on her own. They're looking into it, but it's not priority."

Hannah's jaw drops. "That's insane!"

"That's what I said," I mutter. "But what else can I do?"

"There has to be another way. Kaitlyn wouldn't just leave, and what about her phone that's suddenly disconnected?"

"I mentioned all of that," I say, flopping down onto my mother's luxury couch. "But they only said 'We'll look into it.' They're looking for this Chris guy, but sadly if they can't find him, they won't push it."

"That's so stupid!"

"I know," I say, putting my head in my hands.

"Marlie," she says hesitantly. "There is one other option."

I lift my head and glance at her. "And that would be?"

She bites her lip, then says, "Kenai Michelson."

"Hell no!" I cry, leaping up. "No fucking way am I asking that broody, arrogant, overpriced prick to help me."

She throws her hands on her hips and gives me a hard stare. She might be small, but she's lethal when she wants to be. "You don't even know him. You've never met, and he's the best investigator this side of the country."

"I might not have met him, but everyone knows what he's like. Everyone. I've read the stories about him. He's a horrible person," I point out.

Her lips twitch. "The police could take months, even longer, to find anything. Kenai is amazing. He could find your sister and Chris in half the time."

I shoot her a look. "So you want me to make a deal with the devil?"

She meets my gaze. "I guess it depends on how much you want to find Kaity."

That hits me like a punch to the chest.

"Don't," I warn. "Don't do that, Hannah. You know how much I love her."

She shrugs and raises her hands, then slaps them

to her thighs. "Then go and see him. Yes, he's said to be difficult to work with, but anyone who knows anything says he's the best in his field."

"Didn't he throw a woman out of his car for pissing him off? Like, he literally lifted her up and launched her out of his car, while it was moving."

"You don't know if that's true. Besides I heard it was going like ten miles per hour."

"Hannah!" I cry.

She gives me a soft look. "Think about it, Marlie, you know he can help."

I grunt.

She pats my shoulder.

Dammit, she's probably right.

FOUR

I'm trying one last pathetic attempt at getting information for the police so I don't have to turn to Kenai. Well, I'm *planning* on trying one last pathetic attempt. Right now I'm sitting in my car, trembling, feeling acid burning in the pit of my stomach, staring out at the local café near my home, where all the people I grew up with spend time.

Getting out means facing this town again. Facing the stares. Facing the horrible sympathetic words and attempts at making me feel better. Facing the gawkers, the fans. I don't know if I can do that. My sister's face flashes in my mind and pain crushes my chest. I'm doing this for her. She'd do it for me.

So I swing the door open and get out. I make it halfway down the street when it starts. Random people calling out. Whispering to each other. "Oh my God, is that Marlie Jacobson? What is she doing back in town? Let's go talk to her. Maybe she'll take a picture with us."

Keep your head down. Don't let them in. You can breathe free, Marlie. You can overcome this. You don't have to let this rule your life. You don't have to let this be who you are. This does not need to be your story.

I repeat this mantra in my head over and over as my sneakers pound the cracked footpath below me. My breathing is coming in short, shallow pants and my heart is racing so hard I can feel it in my throat. *Just ignore them. They'll go away. They will. Just get to the café, ask the questions and leave.*

"I can't believe she'd come back here after what that Clayton man did to her. I'd never come back to a place after something like that," I hear.

The name sends a jolt through my body, right to my heart, but I keep moving. My knees ache as I pick up the pace, but I have to overcome this. It doesn't need to rule my life. I'm here to help my sister. I have to think of my sister. *Kaity. Kaity. Kaity.*

"I don't know why she'd want to come back here, now that she's got all that money and is living the dream."

Living the dream.

Living the dream?!

I'm living the nightmare. People will never understand what it was like living through the horror I faced. They'll never understand that their attention made me feel pathetic, and weak. They'll never understand how it felt to walk down the street, wondering if it would happen again, wondering if someone else would hurt me. Living in a constant state of paranoia. Just a few years ago, even going to the store was an ordeal. I'd seize up with panic attacks midway there, and have to turn around and run home in a cold sweat.

No. They'll never understand. They've conjured up images and stories in their minds, they've read news reports, they've decided who they think I am.

I'm the girl who got away.

I'm the girl who slayed the serial killer.

I'm the girl who just wants to disappear.

"No, we know nothing," The café owner, Michael, mutters as he stares at his feet.

He can't even look at me.

I've been in here ten minutes, asking questions, but no one can look me in the eye long enough to answer me. It's like they're afraid of me, like they just don't know what to say. I guess I'd probably be the same, but it's been long enough now that surely they can at least try. Sometimes I wonder if they think I'm going to just lose it on them.

"I just want to know if anyone has seen her," I yell, throwing my hands up. "Is it really so hard to help me? This was my sister's favorite café. if anyone has seen her, it's probably someone here."

Everyone shuffles uncomfortably in their seats, still looking away. The only people who gawk at me are the newcomers or people who don't know who I am. They're simply enjoying the show.

"Marlie," Michael says. "I'll have to ask you to leave. My customers are trying to eat and you're disturbing them."

"And I don't appreciate being treated like a leper."

His face hardens. "Please leave. We can't help you. We haven't seen Kaity."

"No," I grunt, walking towards the door. "You never could, could you?"

I open it and slam it shut, and face the onslaught of gossip again. I put my head down and charge to my truck. When I reach it, I get in, slam the door, and speed off down the street. I make it only a mile or so before I stop on the side of the road, drop my head into my hands, and break out in a cold sweat.

My throat gets tight and I struggle to breathe.

Another panic attack.

I'm used to them now, but that doesn't make it any easier. I try to fight through the constricting pain in my chest to breathe, but the pressure is too much. I start to pant, pressing a hand to my forehead and another to my heart, which is pounding. Tears burn under my eyelids, but I shove them back.

I'm stronger than this.

I force a breath through the pain, then another,

and another, until finally the constriction eases and shaky breaths pass through my lips easier. Thank God. With shaky fingers I manage to focus back on the road. I know what I have to do, and doing it is literally a last resort, but my sister needs me, and I think she deserves someone to sacrifice for her for once.

So I start my car and turn it around, heading straight towards lower downtown Denver.

To Kenai Michelson's office.

FIVE

FIVE

"I would like to see Kenai, if he's in, please," I say to the pretty blonde gawking at me over the reception desk.

"Are you Marlie Jacobson?"

I inwardly sigh. "Yes," I mutter.

"Oh my God," she squeaks. "I just finished your book and it ripped my heart out. I can't believe you survived that."

I force a smile. "Kenai, please?"

She glances nervously to her left, then leans closer and whispers. "Can I have an autograph, I mean, would you mind?"

"Of course," I say, my voice void of emotion. I don't know how she's still smiling. Hell, my voice is so empty it scares me.

She pulls out her copy of *My Encounter with the Devil* and hands it to me. I glare at the cover.

It's some lame creation of a woman's crying eye. The type is bright red and scary. The title, though, is what annoys me the most. It sounds like I had tea with a monster and then skipped merrily home. God, I hate this book. I fucking hate it.

I scribble my name on the inside page and then glare expectantly at the girl. "Kenai?"

"Of course," she gushes, lifting up the phone and pressing it to her ear.

"Yes, Kenai, I have Marlie Jacobson up at reception asking to see you."

Her bright face falls and she nods. "Right, very sorry, sir. I didn't mean to interrupt."

She hangs up the phone and looks over to me. By the upset and bothered look on her face, the stories about Kenai are true. He's a jerk. Great.

"He said he doesn't have time and whatever it is you want, he doesn't want any part of it."

Asshole didn't even hear me out. That's not okay.

"Pick up the phone and dial him again," I order.

"Miss Jacobson, I can't do that—"

"Pick it up," I hiss. "And dial him back, then hand it to me."

"I really . . ."

"Do it or I will."

Her face grows red as she lifts the phone, dialing again. She thrusts it at me, and I give her a weak smile. "I'll tell him I tackled you and got it,"

I say, trying to offer her assurance, considering she looks like she's going to puke.

"I told you I'm fucking busy," comes the deepest, sexiest voice I've ever heard in my life.

"Dismissing someone without even speaking to them is rude," I snap into the phone. "Didn't your mother teach you any manners?"

"Who the fuck is this?"

"Marlic Jacobson, and I'm not leaving until you talk to me."

"Not fuckin' interested."

"Then I'll wait out here until you are, and believe me, I'm a determined woman. Or haven't you read my book?"

He makes a throaty, pissed-off sound and hangs up.

Fine.

I thrust the phone back at the receptionist and walk over to a chair, plonking myself down. I smile at her, cross my legs, and wait. I don't expect him to come out, but less than five minutes later the door swings open and out comes the deadliest, sexiest, roughest man I've ever seen.

Eyes the color of lush, green forest trees swing my way, and I freeze. They're the most incredible eyes, I could get lost in them. Surrounded by thick black lashes. Set amongst olive skin. His jaw is hard, and carries the scars to prove it. His nose is slightly crooked, clearly having been broken a few too many times, but his lips, oh his lips—full and plump and almost delicate.

I've heard a lot about Kenai's good looks, but never did I expect them to be this powerful. There's something about him that makes my body feel weak. He's tall and built like a brick wall. Solid, muscled, and fucking gorgeous. His hair is dark, maybe brown, maybe black. It's hard to tell, but it has little flecks of light brown throughout. It's just long enough that you could run your hands through it. He is boasting the messy I've-not-brushed-it-for-a-few-days look.

He's got a few days' growth on his jaw, and he's dressed all in black, like some badass biker. He's got rings on his fingers, thick ones, skulls maybe, and he's got chains hanging from his pants. His boots are undone. Messy and sexy seems to be his angle. He's got tattoos snaking up his arms and, it would appear, popping back out at his neck.

Hot.

Also an asshole.

"You've got three seconds to get the fuck out of my office before I lift you up and throw you out," he rumbles.

I stand, finding my backbone. "I've heard you like to throw women, but I can assure you, Mr. Michelson, that if you touch me, I'll break your fucking nose." I stare at his nose, then smirk. "Again."

He flinches, but I see a flash of surprise cross his face before he masks it.

"Can't imagine what a girl like you is doin' in my office."

A girl like me. I'd love to know what kind of girl he thinks I am.

"I came for the service you're offering. Shouldn't take a genius to figure that out," I point out sarcastically.

He crosses his arms, and his muscles flex. His face is hard as stone, not breaking even for a second.

"You have two minutes to tell me what you want, or I'll risk getting my nose broken, *again*."

Jerk.

I cross my arms. "I want you to find my sister. There, that only took two seconds."

He keeps his arms crossed, his face blank.

"Are you deaf?" I snap.

"No, just don't think I'm hearin' you right. You want me to find your sister, who has only been missing twenty-four hours and is known to be runnin' around trampin' it up with a bunch of drug lords?"

"How do you know that?"

He gives me a look. "I know everything, Marlie."

My spine straightens. "No you don't, because she is not tramping it up with anyone!"

He glares at me. "I know the ins and outs of this town, and I know what she's been doin'."

"Listen." I step closer. He doesn't move. "I didn't come here to hear how good you are, or what you know. I came here to get your help."

He leans in even closer, and I try not to inhale his masculine, heavenly scent. "I don't take on short cases with no evidence that a person is actually missing."

I lose my cool and poke him in the chest. "Listen, buddy, what the fuck does it matter to you how long she's been missing or if it's an actual fact? I'm offering to pay for your help, so what the hell is the problem?"

He reaches out and takes my finger from his chest, lowering it back down to my side. Swift. "There are real cases out there. Children missing. Wives disappeared. *Those* things matter. *Those* things I take my time out to fuckin' go hunting for, not a sister who is running around getting high with her fuckin' boyfriend."

"She's not," I say through my clenched teeth. "She's in danger."

He shifts from one foot to the other. "And you know this because?"

"I know my sister!" I cry, trying to keep my frustration under control.

"That's not enough of a reason."

Breathe. Marlie. Breathe. "I'll pay you double your going rate."

He cocks an eyebrow. "You think throwing your cheat cash in my face will get me to help you?"

Cheat cash? What the fuck. I take a breath and force myself to stay calm.

"No, I'm not expecting anything. I'm asking a man who is the best at his job to help me because I have no one else."

He stares at me, really stares, then narrows his eyes. "You could hire anyone with the money you got floatin' around. Why me?"

"Like I said, you're the best." I struggle to keep the anger out of my voice. *Don't get pissed off, Marlie. You're nearly there. He's cracking.*

He looks over to the receptionist. "Cases. List them. Now."

"You just cleared up the Smith case," she stammers, flicking through the diary quickly. "You're finishing up the Waters case this week, and then you're due in New York for the missing wife if she hasn't turned up by next month."

Kenai turns back to me and sighs. "Two weeks, that's all I have time for. Better get your checkbook ready, I don't come cheap."

"Thought my cheat cash didn't matter to you," I mutter.

He flashes me a glare. "You want my help? Then you shut it and let me do my job."

"I'm coming with you," I point out.

I know Kenai usually takes someone close to the missing person with him when he does a case, for information, so I know he doesn't really have the grounds to turn me down. I expect him to protest, but instead his eyes light up in a dangerous kind of way. "Then welcome to two weeks of hell. Pack your bags, princess, you're about to see what the real world is about."

Shit.

SIX

"You did it?" Hannah asks, eyes wide.

I rummage through my clothes, making sure I've got everything I need. I just got off the phone with Paul, telling him I needed more time off. He was understanding, and was happy to give it to me. I informed the police of my actions, and because what Kenai does is legal, they took my contact information and told me they would let me know of any changes.

Now I'm preparing myself for time on the road with a jerk of a man. How the hell am I going to cope with two weeks with him? He can barely grunt two words at me as it is, so maybe that's a good thing. We'll be spending twenty-four hours a day together on a road trip; we'll probably be staying in the same places overnight. God. What the hell am I thinking?

Kaitlyn. That's what I'm thinking.

"Yes, he agreed to help me," I mumble, holding up a shirt. Too crinkled? Too old? Who cares. I'm not trying to impress anyone. I toss it in the "take" pile.

"Was he nice about it?"

I give her a look. "Have you ever heard of him being nice about anything?"

She smiles. "No. So how long will you be gone?"

"He said he can give me two weeks. We're going to Kaity's apartment today to see if we can get some info before we hit the road."

"I have Chris's full name, if you need it. And I'll see if I can dig up anything else from people around town before you go."

I smile at her, grateful. "Thanks, Hannah. I don't know what I'd do without you."

She grins. "Probably die."

I chuckle. "Probably."

Hannah wishes me luck, tells me she'll call with any information, and gets going. She said she's going to visit her grandmother for a few days, but she promised to call often. I finish making sure I've got everything I need. With winter coming in the next few weeks, things are cooling down quickly. I only have one jacket. I'll have to get more clothes along the way.

With a sigh, I zip up my suitcase and go downstairs to say goodbye to my mom. Kenai told me he'll be here at three p.m. sharp and if I'm not outside he'll leave. It's 2:50 now. I drop my suitcase at the door and find Mom in the kitchen, drinking wine and staring out the window. Sometimes I wonder if somewhere deep down in her mind, she is struggling, too. Or has the money and fame really just become her everything?

"Hey, Mom," I say and she turns, studying me. "I'm leaving now."

She stands and rushes over, throwing her arms around me. "You're doing such a brave thing for your sister."

I stare up at the ceiling. "Yeah, well, hopefully I'll find her."

"She could be anywhere, enduring anything. Oh, Marlie, I feel like I'm cursed. This is the worst thing a mother could possibly go through. Why is this happening to me?"

Way to make it about you, Mom. She still thinks only about herself. Granted, she's always been this way, but hell, I don't have time for the frustration.

"I have to go," I mutter, turning and walking towards the door.

"Stay safe, Marlie."

"I will, Mom." I lift my suitcase and shove the front door open, stepping out just as a huge, black, chunky-looking truck pulls into the driveway. The window rolls down and I see Kenai sitting in the front seat, his eyes on my mother's house. He's got a scowl on his face, as if the very image of the house makes him feel ill. Yeah, well, I feel the same, buddy.

I walk towards the car, but he throws the door open and gets out, walking around and snatching my suitcase from my hands. He doesn't say a word as he throws it in the back and then opens my door for me to get in. I stare at him, mouth agape, eyes wide. He opens doors but he can't speak a nice word?

"Get in," he grunts.

"You're opening my door," I say, not moving.

"Yeah, it's called fucking manners. Now get in."

I scoff. "Manners? Swearing at a woman isn't manners. I think you've got it all wrong, buddy."

"Get," he growls, leaning down close, "in."

"All right, keep your shirt on."

I leap into his truck as graceful as a gorilla, and he slams the door before walking around the front. I stare at him as he goes, watching the wind whip around the messy hair atop his head. He's wearing all black again, and today his shirt is so tight I can see the outlines of his muscles as he moves.

Hot.

Asshole.

He gets in the driver's side again, then turns to me. "We're going to look at the apartment, but before we do there are rules. I won't drive away until you're clear on them."

I cross my arms. "Hit me then."

He grunts. "First, you do everything I say."

I snort.

He glares.

"I'm fuckin' serious, woman. You do everything I say, when I say it, and you don't argue."

"Does that mean I can't go to the toilet without your permission, Chief?"

His jaw tics. "Second rule," he rasps through clenched teeth. "No sass."

"Can't help the way I am," I point out.

"Then keep it to yourself. I can't guarantee your safety if you don't do as you're told. When we're out somewhere or I'm talking to people, you stay the fuck where I tell you and keep it quiet. You want your sister found, you'll let me do my job and refrain from getting in my way."

"All right, buddy, I get it," I say, throwing my hands up.

"Third rule, you stay in my sight at all times unless we're in a safe location. I don't need a second missing person."

I put my hand to my forehead and salute.

"Fourth rule," he practically spits at me. "You do not ask questions, you do not speak, you do not look at my things. I know what I'm doing, and your opinion means nothing to me."

"I got it." I sigh. "Sit down, be quiet, smile nicely, don't speak."

He growls again.

It's kind of sexy.

No. *Asshole.*

"Now, give me my check before we leave."

I roll my eyes, reach into my bag, and pull out the check. He takes it, glances at the amount, then stuffs it in his pocket and stares straight forward.

He starts the truck and we begin the drive to my sister's apartment.

"Are you broody because of your job, or because you're just an asshole by nature?"

His jaw tics again.

"Rule four amended. No talking . . . *at all.*"

"So we're going on a long road trip, and I can't talk?"

Normally, I'm the furthest thing from a social butterfly. But his rules and hard-ass attitude make me want to mess with him.

His fingers go white around the steering wheel. "Talk in your own head."

"That would mean I have problems."

He snorts. "And you don't?"

"Low blow, Chief."

"My name is Kenai!"

"My name is Kenai," I mumble to myself, turning and staring out the window. "Can I at least sing?"

"No," he barks.

"Hum?"

He makes a deadly sound in his throat as I continue to stare at the passing scenery with a smirk on my face. This could be a little fun.

We drive for another few minutes before I turn and ask, "How much is this trip going to cost me? You're not going to stay in five-star hotels are you?"

"You've got plenty of cash, Miss Devil Wrangler. I'm sure it won't matter."

That annoys me. My chest clenches as I glare at his profile.

"I beg your pardon?"

"Everyone in the world knows who you are, and what you went through. They also know you used that story, that pain, that situation—a situation that so many families just wish their child made it out alive from—to make money. Shitloads of it."

"Is that what you think?" I say, my voice shaky.

"I don't think it, woman. I *know* it."

"Of *course* you do. 'Cause you know more than I do about my situation."

I glance straight ahead, fuming inside but mostly hurting. He assumes he knows me; he assumes he knows how it all went down. He has no idea. But, hey, let the asshole think what he wants.

I don't need him to like me.

I just need to get Kaitlyn back.

A thick lump forms in my throat as I take in my sister's apartment. It's sectioned off with yellow police tape, but Kenai has clearance to go in. He explained that the police allow him access to some evidence after they've done a full sweep, especially if he has been hired to work on a case. The moment we step in, my heart lurches and pain shoots to my very core. The entire place is trashed. Things are strewn about everywhere, lamps and photos are smashed, drawers are completely emptied.

Forgetting Kenai, I start rummaging through

her things. I come across an old photo in a frame. It's a picture of us, before I was taken. I think I was about eighteen. It's when we spent a week on the lake for spring break. We're both smiling in our bright-yellow bikinis, looking like we don't have a care in the world. The frame is smashed, and it looks like someone has crumpled the picture with their hands.

Strange.

I smooth out the picture and tuck it into my pocket, swallowing my emotion and walk through the apartment, looking for Kenai. I find him in her bedroom, going through her drawers. He's tossing things aside, moving rapidly, like he knows what he's looking for. He must sense me behind him, because he starts speaking.

"Found drugs under her mattress, sewn in. Pills. Not sure what as yet, but I'm guessing Ecstasy. A good amount. Police must have missed it. Whoever was looking for her was looking for that. My guess is that she and her boyfriend are on the run because they got themselves into some shit."

"I don't . . ."

I stare at the drugs he's tossed onto the bed, and I don't want to believe it. I don't want to believe Kaitlyn would do something like that. But I wouldn't know, because I haven't been there for her the way I should have.

"Face the facts, woman. Burying your head in the sand isn't going to help."

I say nothing.

"It seems her drawers aren't stirred up, which makes me think she left in a hurry, without clothes. Her toothbrush, hairbrushes, those kinds of things are all still in the bathroom. Go into the kitchen, her office, anywhere that paper can be stored, and see if you can find any notes, numbers, letters, things like that. The cops have already searched her laptop. I'm getting it on my way out of town."

I nod and rush out, starting in the kitchen. I find a few notes there, but nothing that seems to provide information. Still, I take them for Kenai anyway. I move into the office, and everything is in disarray. But in the center of the room there's a desk with a note. It seems almost perfectly placed, which is odd in the upturned room. I pick it up and read the typed words.

Los Angeles. Friday. Trade deal.
Last warning.

Why wouldn't the police have taken this? It seems off. My skin prickles as I turn and rush it back to Kenai. He studies the note, narrowing his eyes, flipping it over in his hands a few times. "Where was this, you say?"

"Just sitting on the desk. Almost too perfectly."

"Odd. Cops should have taken it. Makes me think someone came in after them. Either way, it's a start. I'll report it to them and we'll head towards Los Angeles. I've found a few names and numbers we can look into on the way. I interviewed a couple of people before I collected you—the cops have given me as much as they can, but there isn't much here for us. We need to get on the road. Let's go."

"Where are we going first?"

He waves a hand. "This name and number connect to Santa Fe. That's our first stop."

I sigh.

Here we go.

SEVEN

The first few hours of the trip are awful. I sit in awkward silence, wondering if I've made a massive mistake. Can I truly trust this man? And what if I can't? What if I'm going in the wrong direction, wasting precious time? My nerves get the better of me and I tap my fingers on my knees until Kenai barks at me to stop fidgeting. I close my eyes and focus on how I feel inside. I know Kenai's a jerk, but my gut tells me he's the right jerk for the job. I've learned to trust my gut.

Besides, this is for Kaity. It isn't about me. I'd go to the ends of the earth and hire anyone needed to make sure she came home safe. Thinking about her has my chest tightening and an all too familiar anxiety clutching at my heart. What will I do if something happens to her? The thought of her suffering, of her life being cut short . . . No. I can't think like that. I take a deep breath and try to distract myself.

I reach over to turn the radio up, but before my fingers can even reach the dial they're being slapped away. Kenai likes to drive in pure silence, but he had allowed me to turn the radio on. However, he made it so quiet I can't hear the damned thing, just a slight noise. The sun has just set and we have over three hours to go before we stop for the night. I'm not allowed to turn the interior light on to read, so I'm stuck sitting here, in the dark, in silence.

Fine. I'll distract myself by annoying the hell out of him.

"How old are you, Chief?"

He doesn't answer.

"I'll guess. Fifty-two?"

I chuckle at my own joke, but he says nothing. God, he has zero personality.

"I'll keep talking until you answer me. Believe me, I'm not easily silenced."

"Thirty-three," he grunts.

"So young to be so broody."

He snorts.

"Are you married? No wait, I take that back—you're too mean. You might be good-looking, but honestly, that just isn't enough to cover your attitude."

"Are you finished?"

I grin. Surely he knows I'm teasing him, right? Perhaps he's never had a woman take his moods without getting upset. "Are you going to let me turn the radio up?"

He sighs angrily. "Fine."

He turns it up just enough, and I instantly start singing along happily. I throw my feet up on the dash, and he quickly reaches over, jerking them down. I keep singing, a little loudly, and after a few minutes he slams his hand over the volume button, turning it off.

"Hey!" I protest. "I was listening to that!"

"You were singing and it sounded like a cat drowning."

I cross my arms. "How am I supposed to improve without any practice?"

He doesn't answer.

"Are you going to throw me out of the car next?"

"Keep flapping your mouth at me, I will. Ask the last girl how that worked out for her."

"I'd like to see you even try to throw me out of this car. I might be small, but I will give a good damned fight."

He sighs. I'm frustrating him. Good.

"Fine, I'll sit here in silence, wallowing in self-pity, feeling like no one cares . . ."

"God, woman!" he barks as I secretly smile at my dramatics. "Will you just stop fucking talking."

I huff and turn, staring out the window. My knees are already starting to ache and we're barely three hours in. By the time we stop, I'll be in pain, I know I will. If I don't move enough, the pain will get worse and worse until I'm forced to take strong painkillers. In my rush to pack, I didn't think to bring painkillers. I'm sure G.I. Joe next to me has some, at least I hope he does.

I shift uncomfortably.

"Stop squirming. Can't you sleep or something?" Kenai grumbles.

"Do you have any painkillers?"

"Why?"

"I need some."

"What for?" he demands.

I shift again. "They take away pain, do they not?"

"That depends on the kind of pain, certain things work for different areas and problems."

"You know what," I grunt, shifting so I can press my cheek to the window. "Forget about it."

He doesn't say anything.

Neither do I.

It's going to be a long trip.

I'm in agony.

By the time we arrive at a motel, I want to curl up and die. Pain is radiating from my knees, right down to my toes and it hurts. God, does it hurt. Kenai checks us in. There was only one room left, but thankfully it has two beds. Kenai didn't argue—he said he wants to keep an eye on me. Whatever, he's just a control freak. I really wanted my own room and my own scorching-hot shower, but I'm in too much pain to argue.

The nerves grow worse as I watch him carry in our bags while I try not to hobble towards the entrance. What if I have a nightmare? I don't want him to hear that. Maybe I should go back and request adjoining rooms. Surely they have one spare . . . I reach the front door and step through the open space to see Kenai digging through the bag he's thrown on a nice enough double bed. One of two.

I move as quickly as I can to my bed and sit down. My knees scream at me and I start to shake a little. Hot water is what I need, and hopefully I can steal some painkillers from Kenai's bag when he showers. I stand and keep my eye on him as I grab a towel and walk towards the bathroom. I feel his burning gaze on my back, but I don't turn. I just step in and shut the door.

The moment I'm alone, I place my hands on the basin and lean over, taking some deep breaths. It'll be fine. I'm so tired I won't dream and if I do I'm sure he won't notice. I don't usually scream. *Usually*. My knees will feel better after a hot shower. Everything is going to be just fine. I'm doing this for Kaity. She needs me and I have to keep reminding myself of that.

I push back and hobble over to turn on the shower. I strip out of my clothes and step under the water. I make it as hot as I can take it, lean against the cool tiled wall, and let the water run over my slightly outstretched knees. They hurt, God, do they hurt. The damage that was done to them can never be undone: ligaments, muscles, bones—all destroyed. I stare down at the ugly scars surrounding them and their odd shape.

Horrible. Ugly. Disgusting.

My eyes flicker to my wrists, where faded scars are still visible. Most people think they are from self-inflicted wounds, but in reality they are from when I was bound. I tried so hard to get out that I tore apart my own skin. Most people don't notice the scars because I wear a watch and bracelets, but they're there. A constant reminder of the horror I endured. Then there's my hair and the way it looks because of all the hair he ripped out of my head. I fix my hair to cover it now, but there are still patches where no hair has grown back.

Wincing in pain, I manage to wash myself before getting out and drying off. It's then I realize I didn't bring in a change of clothes, and the ones I was wearing are now damp from the non-existent shower curtain in the shower. Great. Just great. I tuck the faded-green towel around myself and open the door, peering out. Kenai is standing by the window on his phone, shirtless.

I suck in a breath.

Mother of God.

He's huge. A big wall of muscled man. His skin pulls and stretches over muscles that are so bulky, I can see every curve and fine line. His skin is smooth and covered in tattoos. Intricate designs that don't really seem to represent anything but are beautiful all the same. His jeans hang low on his narrow hips and his long, thick legs seem to go on forever. Dark hair curls around his neck and, I can't deny it, the back of him is an amazing sight.

I sneak out towards my bag, but my knees are killing me and each step gets harder and harder. A good night's sleep should help. The floorboards squeak and Kenai spins around. I'm taken off guard by his ripped body and the tattoos covering his chest, and he's taken off guard because I'm half naked trying to creep towards my bag. His eyes drop to my towel, then lower to my knees.

I know I'm standing funny but I can't help it. I'm in pain.

I shift uncomfortably, because I know he's looking at my scars. I turn my back to him and take some clothes from my bag, then hobble back to the bathroom. I dress as quickly as I can and then step back out. By the time I reappear, Kenai is off the phone and has a towel thrown over his shoulder. The moment I step out, he stops and glances at me again.

"You're in pain."

"I told you that already," I mutter, throwing my covers back. "But you wanted twenty questions instead of just giving me what I need."

He nods at my knees. "Those give you trouble often?"

"Considering they were smashed, yes."

His eyes flick up to mine. "Smashed?"

"Come off it. Don't pretend you don't know.

You seem to assume you know everything about me, but you don't know that—" My voice changes. I swallow. "—he broke my knees and smashed them up?"

"I didn't know that."

He doesn't say any more, but he walks to his bag, leans down, ruffles about, and pops back up with a strip of white pills in his hands. He thrusts them at me and I catch them, meeting his eyes. "Those will help. I'm having a shower."

"Thanks," I mutter as he disappears.

It's early and somehow I have to try and distract myself in a room with him until it's time for bed. I grab my phone, climb onto my bed, and plug in my earphones.

It's going to be a long few hours.

EIGHT

My vision is blurred. I glance around, trying to figure out where I am, but I'm bound. I blink a few times, but the room is so dark I can't see a single thing. I can't hear anything. I don't know where I am. My mind works back to the hours leading up to this point. I helped a man who dropped his briefcase, then . . . hazy memories of waking up bound in the back of a van, then . . . nothing.

I jerk on my restraints, but my hands are firmly fastened behind my back and my ankles are bound together. I wiggle and shuffle until I'm sitting up. I'm on the ground, concrete from the feel of it. I don't risk calling out, not wanting to alert whoever has taken me that I'm awake. Fear clogs my chest and I try to steady my breathing.

Have I been kidnapped? Am I going to get sold? Raped? Worse?

I groan at the sharp pain that radiates through my stomach, letting me know my fear is very real and very present. A sound clicks to my left and some light enters the room. A man walks in. He's holding something in his hand, but I don't know what. He looks completely normal—dark hair, blue eyes, average height.

Who is he?

"I see you're awake," he murmurs, pushing the door open even further, then flicking on a light.

It takes my eyes a few seconds to adjust. When they do, I glance at him again then drop my gaze to the item in his hand. It looks . . . like hair. My stomach coils tightly as he laughs loudly, stepping closer.

"Don't you like my trinket?"

He holds the hair up. It's the same color as mine. There are bloodstains in it. I'm going to be sick. Oh God. I'm going to be sick. Who is this guy and what does he want from me? God. Help.

"Let me go," I plead, brokenly.

He chuckles. "Not even a scream? The other girls screamed when they realized who I was."

Who is he?

I don't understand.

"Ah," he smirks, running his finger through the hair. "You don't know who I am."

Say nothing.

Try and find a way out.

There has to be a way.

"I'm sure you've heard of me. What was that name they gave me in the media? Oh yes. The Watcher."

The Watcher.

Fear slams into my chest and my world starts spinning as everything I heard about that name comes rushing back to me. The man who takes girls and skins them alive. Serial killer. I remember hearing it on the news and knowing they were not even close to figuring out who he is.

No.

God. Please. No.

I scream and try to break free of my binds. They're so tight, my wrists burn. I don't stop.

"Ah, now we're really getting somewhere. Here." *He tosses the hair and it lands on my lap. My screams become frantic as I stare at the tattered mess. Is that . . . is that skin? "This is from the last girl. Weak one she was. No fun at all. You on the other hand." He steps in closer, grinning. "You look like you're going to be so much fun."*

I jerk upright with a gasp, hands automatically going to my lap where they flick a nonexistent object away. Sweat trickles down my brow and it takes me a moment or two to gather my bearings. I glance around the dark room, rubbing my chest to try and ease my pounding heart, then remember where I am and who I'm with.

Kenai.

Looking for Kaitlyn.

It's all just fine.

I swallow down the burning sensation in my throat, and slowly flick my covers back and glance over at Kenai's bed. He's facing the wall on his side, arm tucked up under his head. His back practically glistens under the moonlight streaming in from the crack in the curtains. I carefully tiptoe to the tiny fridge in the corner and open it, grabbing a bottle of water.

I take it back to my bed, and stretch my knees as I move. They're feeling better—whatever Kenai gave me was good. I sit back down on the side of the bed and sip the water, enjoying the soothing effect it has on my throat. I close my eyes and sigh quietly. It was just a dream. *He's gone. He's dead. I survived.* I repeat this mantra in my head until a husky, sleepy voice croaks, "How bad was it?"

I jerk and look over at Kenai's bed. He's still facing the wall, but he's obviously awake. My heart starts pounding. So he did hear me? Was I screaming? God, what did I say?

"Sorry. I didn't mean to wake you," I whisper into the darkness.

"The dream. How bad?"

"Ah, it's fine."

"Wasn't fine," he grunts, rolling over and glancing at me. I try very hard to keep my eyes off his chest, but it's hard. I haven't been with a man since I was taken—five years ago. Before that, I was somewhat of a wild child and quite popular. I had a couple of boyfriends, but nothing serious. I enjoyed being young and free. "You were screaming for ten solid minutes."

And he just laid there?

"Sorry."

"Wasn't going to wake you up. They say that isn't a good thing. You stopped only a minute or two ago."

"Sorry," I say again.

He sits up, running a hand through his hair. Don't look.

"Stop apologizing. Not going to talk about it?"

I narrow my eyes. "You think you know everything about me. You've come to your own conclusions and made your own assumptions. What makes you think I'd talk about it with you?"

He glowers at me. "Have it your way."

I clamp my mouth shut. Angry and a little disappointed that he didn't even try to argue that he wanted to know. What did I expect? He's only asking how I am because it's clearly the right thing to do. I lay back down, pulling the cover over my body and listening until Kenai starts deep breathing again.

He went back to sleep.

Just like that.

This is going to be a long trip.

Even before the sun comes up the next morning, Kenai is dressed and ready to hit the road. I drag myself out of bed, groaning with frustration as my legs refuse to let me move around without pain. Still, I manage to get dressed, grunt at Kenai when he asks if I want coffee, and then follow him to the truck.

We hit the road in silence and I actually doze off a bit as we head into Santa Fe. Kenai wants to go to a club to speak with a man about Chris. This is where our first lead is, so we're going to follow it in hopes we get some answers. I don't know how the two are connected, but Kenai has been on the phone for a few hours, tracking down information. The club owner is apparently well known in the drug industry.

I guess it's a better lead than we could've had staying in Colorado.

We arrive at the club just past noon, after getting breakfast and waiting for Kenai to make some more calls. The club is above a restaurant and bar, and apparently is a part of it. The restaurant and bar are open, but the club is closed. Kenai has it on good authority that the owner is here, though. At least, that's what I gathered from his conversations. Outside of his talking on the phone, he's barely said a word to me.

Whatever.

Kenai parks the truck in an alley next to the club/restaurant and turns to me, face stern. "Do not get out of this truck."

I salute him. "Yes Chief."

His jaw tics. "I mean it, Marlie. I don't have time

for any shit. You stay in this truck or you'll have me to answer to."

"I heard you the first time," I mutter.

He glares at me, then gets out, slamming the door and locking the truck with a click of the keys. I sit tight because I don't want to anger the beast this early. I wait for a solid thirty minutes before Kenai finally returns, face tight, fists clenched. He unlocks the car and leaps in, starting it up with an angry grunt.

"What happened?"

"Don't speak to me."

I cross my arms. "That wasn't one of the rules. It's my sister. I'm paying you. Answer me."

He shoots a look at me and grinds out, "My contact wasn't there. Somehow the fucker knew I was coming. I don't have any idea how he found that out. Did you tell anyone?"

I shake my head. "Who the hell would I tell that would know him?"

He rubs a hand over his face. "Either way. I know where he is. Buckle up, princess. We're going to Vegas."

I blink. "Pardon me?"

"I didn't stutter."

"Vegas is like nine hours away."

"We'll stop on the way."

"You can't be serious. We're going all that way to talk to someone who may or may not have information about Chris?"

"That's where this fuck is going to be for the

next week, and he's the best lead we have. So if we want to find him, we need to get moving. Do you want to find your sister or not?"

"Yes, but . . ."

"Then don't question how I do my job," he says, pulling the truck out onto the main highway. "You just do what I say. *Please*. Now buckle up."

"My God, do you always have to be such an asshole? I have a right to know where you are taking me and what the plan is."

"Yeah," he mutters. Then after a pause he continues. "We'll go to Flagstaff tonight, then onto Vegas tomorrow. I have another lead in Flagstaff that's connected to this guy—he might be able to give us more information."

"Great," I mumble, tucking my legs up and staring out the window. Fortunately, they seem to be adjusting to my new routine. They don't hurt nearly as much as they did yesterday.

Kenai says nothing as we hit the road for another long journey. I fall asleep somewhere around two in the afternoon and don't wake for several hours. When I do, the sun is beginning to drop on the horizon and Kenai, as always, is focused solely on the road. I can't do this no-speaking business any longer.

"You might not like me—" I begin after rubbing my eyes and stretching.

"I don't."

God. Jerk.

"I didn't even finish what I was going to say!"

"Don't care to hear what you were going to say."

Anger bubbles in my chest and I snap, "What is your problem with me?"

He says nothing.

"Are you secretly attracted to me, is that it?"

His fingers tighten around the wheel and he snaps, "No, I'm not fuckin' attracted to you."

"Then what's the problem? Are you like this with everyone or is it just me?"

He doesn't answer.

I growl in frustration.

"You know, I think you judge people too harshly. You don't even give them a chance."

He doesn't answer for a second, then says, "What?"

"You don't give people a chance. You just assume to know everything about them."

"Wrong," he mutters.

"Spare me your crap. I know what you think. It's the same thing everyone else thinks."

"And that would be?"

"That I used my situation to make millions."

His jaw tics, and I know I'm right.

"Didn't you?"

"Is that what you think?"

He glances at me quickly, then mutters, "Seen the book. Seen the house. Yeah. That's what I think."

"And you think I'm selfish because I did that."

He has no idea. None. But I'll play his little game.

"Fuck yeah, I think it's selfish. Those other girls

never got a second chance, and instead of relishing in your freedom, you make money from it. And their families have to see it and be reminded of everything they lost, all so you can make a buck."

"Let me tell you something," I say, my voice a low angry growl. "You know—"

I don't get to finish, because out of the blue, a loud bang sounds out. The truck rocks to the side, and for a moment I'm confused and a little dazed. It takes a second more to realize what's happening when another bang sounds out and Kenai curses. Are we being shot at? Oh. Oh my God. We're being shot at!

"Kenai!" I cry, frantically. "Is someone shooting at us?"

He looks behind us, and I follow his vision. A black SUV with dark windows is there. There is no one else around. How did we miss that car creeping up on us? But most importantly, why the hell are they shooting at us? The window winds down and an arm comes out. Another shot sounds out, this one hitting the tire.

I scream.

"Grab the wheel!" Kenai bellows.

"What?" I gasp, shaking my head and throwing my hands up. "No."

"Now!" he roars.

I reach over and grab the wheel without thought. The truck swerves when Kenai spins around, bumping my arm as he reaches into the back and pulls out . . . is that a gun?

"Oh my God, you have a gun!?"

"Shut up and focus," he barks.

Oh shit. This isn't good.

He lowers the window, leans out, and starts shooting. The truck sways as I try to steer around him, which is really hard when you're being shot at and your tires are in less-than-desirable condition. The blasts of the gun hurt my ears, and it takes everything I have inside to stay focused on the road ahead. Kenai shoots again and the SUV behind us speeds up.

Panic seizes my chest and I feel as though I'm going to stop breathing.

"Kenai," I squeak without thought.

"Hang on to the wheel, keep it steady no matter what happens. Focus, Marlie."

I swallow the fear and focus on the road. The SUV comes closer to our side. Another shot rings out and the truck swerves. I scream as Kenai slams his foot on the brake and we start spinning out of control. I try to keep the car as straight as possible but there's no point, it won't happen. We skid off the side of the road, hitting the dust and coming to a screeching halt.

Kenai leaps out of the truck before I even have a chance to take a shaky, relieved breath.

When the dust clears, I see we're alone. Completely alone. The SUV has gone and the roads are empty. Kenai bellows a curse to no one in particular, then comes around to my side of the truck, jerking the door open. "You okay?"

I stare at him, blinking, confused. "Ah . . ."

"You're bleeding."

I shake my head, confused. "What?"

"You must have hit your head. Get out."

I reach up and touch my forehead. My fingers come back covered in blood, and my entire body goes stiff. Oh. Oh God. Memories flood my mind and I tremble as I stare at the sticky blood. I remember another time my head was bleeding. Oh. Oh. Oh God.

His fingers curl into my hair as he drags me down the hall. I fight, but my body is tired and weak. He hasn't fed me for two days. I've had minimal water. He's been torturing me with stories of what he's going to do. Today he's going to show me a video. A video of him skinning his last victim alive.

I can't watch it.

I won't.

I fight some more, trying to release myself from his hold. It's pointless. He's too strong and I'm too weak. He tugs my hair and I scream. I try to lash out, which only angers him more. He slams my head down onto the ground so hard my vision blurs as pain explodes behind my eyes. A broken scream is ripped from my throat as he lifts me and starts jerking me down the hall again.

Something warm trickles down my face.

Blood.

"The first drop of blood," he says, stopping and reaching down, wiping it off with his finger. It

comes back red and I gag at the sight. He raises it and brings it to his mouth.

No.

Don't.

He sucks my blood from his finger.

"I can't wait to see how much you bleed. Some bleed more than others, I think you'll be one of them. You just wait until you see the blood pooling around your body as I peel your skin from it."

I gag and sob at the same time.

"I can't wait to show you this movie. The last girl really screamed. She made it so much fun. She bled a lot. I hope you're not squeamish."

He laughs to himself, like he's just said the funniest thing in the world.

"Let me go," I plead for the millionth time.

He ignores it. Clearly tired of answering.

Someone help.

"Marlie!"

Someone is shaking me. I blink rapidly. My heart is pounding, my chest clenching so hard I can't breathe. Another shake has my teeth snapping together and my eyes focusing. Kenai is in front of me, hands on my shoulders, shaking me just enough to snap me out of my memory.

"K-K-Kenai?" I whisper.

"You freaked out."

"I . . ." I stare down at my bloody finger. "It's the blood. Please, get it off."

He reaches for my hand and tucks it behind my back. "Don't look at it. I'll clean it up."

I nod and stare straight ahead at the vast empty, dusty earth and try to focus back on the here and now. Let it go. He's gone. He's dead. I do a few breathing exercises my therapist taught me, and by the time Kenai returns I'm feeling less . . . *freaked out*.

"You okay?" he asks in a thick voice, placing a small first aid kit beside me and pulling out some alcohol wipes.

He takes my hand and wipes the blood off first, then gets to work on my head. The wipes sting, and I close my eyes against the pain.

"Yeah," I mumble.

"That happen often?"

"What?"

"Flashbacks."

I clench my teeth and say nothing.

I focus on the work he's doing on my forehead. I realize his hand is cupping my jaw as he turns my head from side to side to clean it. Suddenly, that's all I can focus on. His hands are big, a little rough, and so masculine. They feel good. Safe even. I open my eyes and see his are focused on my lips. My heart pounds against my rib cage as the air grows thick with a tension I've never felt before.

The second he realizes I'm looking, he lets me go and steps back. "You're done. Just a superficial scratch."

I look anywhere but at him. What was that? A moment? No. He hates me. He's an asshole. But, seriously, what the hell was it?

"What happened to the SUV?" I ask, deciding to change the subject entirely.

He closes the first aid kit and stands back, arms crossed. "Sped off."

"Why would anyone be trying to kill us?" I say, more than confused.

"They weren't trying to kill us."

I blink. "They were shooting at us, Chief."

He shoots me a look. I ignore it and cross my arms, waiting for him to elaborate.

"If they were trying to kill us, they would have shot through the back windscreen, or shot at us when they came past. They were only aiming for the tires, which means their goal was to slow us down."

Oh.

That makes sense.

"Do you think it was ordered by that club owner?"

"Possibly, but that seems extreme. No one seemed to know anything back in Santa Fe, so I don't see how it's related."

"So what could it be?"

He runs his hands through his hair in frustration. "No fuckin' clue. I'm thinking."

"How many tires are out?"

"Two."

"Oh."

"Yeah," he grunts.

"We only have one spare, right?"

He nods, turning and cursing under his breath

again. "And there's no cell reception out here to call a tow."

"Do we wait for a car to come past and help then?"

"Yeah, I guess. Could be hours. Could be minutes."

"I'm sure someone will come past soon," I say hopefully because the idea of spending a night out here terrifies me.

"They probably will, but not everyone will stop."

He makes a good point. I'm not sure I'd stop if I saw two people sitting in the middle of an open highway with gun damage to their tires. Not to mention, Kenai is a scary-looking man. I wouldn't be in a hurry to help him.

"So what do we do?"

He walks to the back of the truck and drops the tailgate down, sitting on it. "We wait."

I slide out of the truck and go over to join him on the tailgate. We sit in silence for the next half an hour, hoping for a car to come past. The sun keeps setting on the horizon. It'll be dark soon. My stomach grumbles and in the silence out here, Kenai hears it.

"Have you got some food?" I ask when he stares at me.

"No."

"Who doesn't bring food on a road trip?"

He glares at me. "We stopped not that long ago for food."

"So? You should still bring some with you, for the drive."

He keeps glaring at me.

"Stop glaring at me," I snap. "The wind will change and your face will stay like that. Oh wait, too late."

I jump down from the tailgate and go to my side of the truck, pulling out my phone. I see I've got two missed calls from Hannah. Praying its news that Kaity is home and safe, I listen to the voice message she left.

"Hey, honey. It's just me. I wanted to see how you were doing. I got your text earlier. I hope everything is okay. No news here about Kaity. I'm still visiting Grams. I'll call you tomorrow and see how things are going. I really hope your trip isn't too eventful."

"Eventful" would be an understatement. I hang up the phone and toss it back into my purse. No service out here so there's no point in trying to call her back. I lean down and dig through it, praying I've got some stashed food, but I come up with nothing more than a tampon, tissues, a key, and a dried flower. Honestly. I don't even want to know how that got there.

With a sigh, I join Kenai again, who is still staring into the distance.

"How can you sit for so long in silence?"

I slide onto the tailgate again and wait for him to answer.

"Not everyone needs to hear their own voice twenty-four hours a day."

Rude.

"I don't like my own voice that much. Believe it or not, when I'm at home I spend a lot of time in silence."

"What, writing the sequel to your encounter with the devil?"

I flinch. Anger and frustration bubble in my chest and I explode without thought. "I didn't write that fucking book, you jerkoff."

He looks to me, shock registering on his face for a second before he turns back and keeps staring. "Doesn't matter if you wrote it or not, you still allowed it to be published and you certainly didn't say no to the money."

I hate his judgment. I should correct him, but I'm so pissed that he assumes he knows everything, I don't. Let him believe what he wants about me. I don't care. I don't need any more judgment in my life.

"I'm going to try and get some sleep in the truck," I say, my voice tight.

He doesn't answer.

"If a car comes, make sure you call out," I mutter sarcastically. "I'm sure you can stand your own voice for a few seconds."

His mouth forms a straight line. "I think there is a rule about your sass."

"There is," I say nonchalantly. "But as you've clearly learned by now, I don't follow rules."

"Clearly," he mutters.

"Deal with it. You're getting paid double. It should be me making the rules."

He shakes his head and looks at me. I hold his gaze with an equally powerful glare.

"Go to sleep. You're pissing me off."

"Oh my," I say in a chipper voice. "That would be something new. You know, Chief, if you ever laughed, I'd probably drop dead from shock."

"If I knew it was that easy, I would have laughed days ago."

I narrow my eyes at him. "I hope you fall off that tailgate and break your leg."

He grunts.

"Jerk."

NINE

A nice old couple stops and gives Kenai a ride to the closest town to get new tires. I stay behind, reading a book on my phone while I wait. I can't believe he left me out here alone, but I say nothing.

When they return him two hours later, he gets to work putting the tires on using only a flimsy flashlight to see by. I try to help, but he barks at me to let him do it. With a frustrated growl, I sit on the side of the road and wait. When he's done, he tells me to get in the truck and we hit the road.

We drive well into the night and arrive in Flagstaff at some ungodly hour. We check into a cheap hotel and both of us crash without even having a shower, we're that exhausted. We sleep until ten the next morning and then grab a fast-food breakfast from a drive-through on our way to Vegas.

He drives on as we devour our deliciously greasy

egg sandwiches and hash browns and seems to be in a better mood today. I throw my feet up onto the dashboard and pop the last bite of hash brown into my mouth.

Once I finish chewing, I ask, "Why are you so angry all the time?"

He doesn't answer.

I sigh and continue. "Seriously, did something bad happen in your life to make you this way or are you just like this because you have to be?"

"My life is none of your business," he says in a low, gravelly tone.

"Maybe not, but would it kill you to speak to me like a human being for five minutes?"

He glances at me from the corner of his eye, then sighs and says, "I have to be this way."

"Because of the job?"

He sighs. "Because of the people I have to encounter. You can't even imagine the shit I have to put up with. The amount of times I've sat in this same situation, answering the same questions, putting up with people I don't know in my space constantly, I have to be like this or I'll go fucking crazy."

"Then why take them with you when you're searching?"

"Because people closest to the ones I'm looking for have information that could take weeks to get on my own. Sometimes they don't even know it until a certain sight or a random comment brings up a memory that turns out to be crucial to the search. I don't take family members unless I have to, but in a case like this, it makes my job easier."

"You leave me in the truck ninety percent of the time. I fail to see how it makes your job easier," I point out.

"You have information I need, you can recognize faces, you can answer questions I might have and help provide background information. You know your sister a lot better than I do, and I want to draw on that information."

"Fair enough. So when you're at home, and not working, are you still this moody?"

He shakes his head a little. "Yeah."

"Imagine how your girlfriends must feel," I mumble half to myself.

"Don't have time for girlfriends."

"Well," I snort. "That's apparent. Even if you did, they'd likely murder you before you even got through the first date."

"Even if I did," he grinds out, "there wouldn't be a first date, so it wouldn't matter."

"So what, you don't date?"

"No."

"What do you do then?"

"I fuck."

A blush creeps up into my cheeks and I turn and look out the window.

He makes a sound that I'd pass off as a chuckle if I didn't know better.

"If I knew all I had to do was say something

about sex to get you to be quiet, I would have done that when we first started."

"I'm just admiring the view," I say, staring at the empty, bland scenery.

"Some view," he murmurs.

I spin around. "I'm not afraid of sex talk, thank you very much."

"That so?" he says, glancing at me again.

"Yeah, that's so."

"So if I tell you that I'd like to bend you over the front of this truck and put my mouth between your legs, licking your pussy until you scream, you wouldn't be at all concerned?"

My cheeks burn, like fire. I haven't had sex for a long time, but more than that, I haven't *ever* spoken to a man that's so bold. I try to take a steadying breath, but nothing comes out. He looks to me, and his face splits into a grin. It's the first time I've seen him actually smile. It takes my breath away like a punch to the chest. I swear if I wasn't sitting in a chair I'd reel backwards with the force of his beauty.

"Thanks for giving me your weakness. Now when you're talking too much I know how to shut you up."

Mouth, why won't you work? You're letting me down in my time of need!

He turns back to the road and I say nothing, because frankly, it's been too long and if I throw a comeback at him now, I'll sound stupid. I tuck my legs to my chest and gaze out the window until we roll into Vegas in the early afternoon. We stop and grab another meal before checking into yet another hotel. We can't go into the club where we're looking for this guy until evening, so I decide to go down and play at the casino for a little while. I could use a distraction.

That's the best part of Vegas, you don't have to leave your hotel to have a bit of fun. I enter the casino and get myself a drink before putting some coins into the slot machines and sitting down. I do this for about an hour, winning not a single thing. The old woman beside me cleans up.

"I knew I should have gotten that one," I murmur to myself as she exclaims happily to herself over her win.

"I thought the same thing."

I spin around and see a gorgeous blond male standing beside me, staring down with a huge smile on his face. I don't know who he is, but he's incredibly good-looking.

"I always pick the wrong ones," I grin. "It doesn't matter what I do."

"Me too," he extends his hand. "My name is Jacob. What's yours?"

"Marlie."

He smiles.

"Yes, I know, like the dog."

His smile gets bigger. "I think it's a beautiful name. It suits you."

"You wouldn't know." I smile back. "You don't know me."

"I'd like to try. Can I buy you a drink?"

Why the hell not?

"Sure."

I stand and follow him to the bar, where he orders me a vodka soda. We take a seat at the bar and I turn to him and say, "So Jacob, do you live in Vegas or are you just visiting?"

"Visiting. You?"

"Same. I'm only stopping in for the night."

His eyes find mine. "Then I had better do a good job at charming you."

I laugh. "You're good, I'll give you that much."

"I have to say, I noticed you the moment I walked in."

I scrunch up my nose. "I can't imagine why."

"Well, there you were, sitting in jeans and a tank top while everyone around you is dressed to the nines. I stood and watched you laughing to yourself as you played. You have these cute little indents in your nose when you smile. It's adorable."

I flush. "So my jeans worked in my favor for once?"

"I'd go with yes. Keep wearing them."

My heart flutters. I haven't flirted with a male since, well, since before *him*.

"Tell me about yourself, Marlie."

I stare at him, and for the first time in a long time, I realize I'm just Marlie. Not the girl who survived. Not the murderer of a serial killer. Not a famous author. Just Marlie. I can be anyone right now. Anyone I want. I'll never see him again.

"There isn't much to tell," I say, and God, that feels good. "I'm just a girl who lives in Colorado Springs and works as a waitress. That's basically it."

He sips his drink, studying my lips. "I think you're more than that."

"Nope." I shrug. "That's me. Just plain old Marlie."

He reaches forward, tucking a strand of hair behind my ear. "You're more than plain and you're certainly not old."

I shiver.

"Yo, hands off."

I flinch at the sound of Kenai's angry voice. I turn and see him standing next to us, arms crossed, glaring at Jacob. God, he's such an asshole. Jacob drops his hand and looks up at Kenai, then back to me, then back to Kenai. "Sorry man, I didn't realize she was taken."

"I'm not."

"She is."

We say it at the same time.

What the hell kind of game is he playing?

"No. Right now he works for me, and if he keeps up his attitude, he won't be for much longer," I snap defiantly.

"Well if that's the case, I guess I'll get in my truck and go home."

Kenai pivots and starts striding out. The damned jerk will likely do just that. "I'm so sorry," I say to Jacob, before leaping up and rushing after Kenai.

"Seriously," I snap when we reach the door. "What is your problem?"

He spins around, pinning me with those intense eyes. "We're here to work, not party and get laid."

"Excuse me, but you told me we weren't going out until later and I wasn't getting laid, I was having a drink."

"That would lead to you getting fucked. I saw how he was looking at you."

"Jealous?" I goad.

He takes a step forward, and I have to stop myself taking one back. Hold your own, Marlie.

"Jealous that I could be getting my fuckin' dick sucked and drinking, instead of doing this shit? Then yeah. So, sweetheart"—he leans in close—"if I'm not getting laid, then neither are you."

I huff. "You can't stop me."

He leans down, drops his shoulder into my belly and launches me into the air. "Watch me."

"Put me down!" I squeal, slapping his back.

God, it's hard. Like a wall, a stone wall.

"Let me go . . . you . . . you . . . behemoth!" I cry out, continuing to pummel his back.

He really does have a nice back. Part of me, even though I don't really want to admit it, is flattered that he's carrying me out of here. It feels nice to know I've gotten a reaction out of him, that he doesn't like me talking to other men. Childish as it may seem, it's been a long time since someone showed such a reaction. It feels nice. But I'm not going to let him know that.

He carries me out of the casino and all the way up to our room. He unlocks the door, walks in, and throws me onto the bed. Then he stalks towards the adjoining doors, looks back at me as he says, "Leave this room and I'm off the case."

Then he steps through and shuts the door behind him.

"Seriously!" I yell, throwing my hands up.

He doesn't come back in.

Kenai is supposed to get me just after six o'clock so we can go over to the club, find this guy, and get some information. I take a shower, get changed, and dry and straighten my hair. I decide to opt out of heavy makeup and apply just a light coat. Then I sit on my bed to wait for him. While I wait, I call Hannah to see if she's heard anything new. She answers on the second ring.

"Hi," she says, sounding puffed.

"You been running or something?" I laugh.

"Or something. How's it going?"

"Not great. We're in Vegas, just about to go to this club and check out a lead. So far, we've had nothing."

I choose not to tell her about the shooting, because honestly, it'll only freak her out more.

"So nothing eventful?" she asks, and I can hear the sounds of shuffling on the other end.

"No, nothing. How are you? How's your gram?"

"She's fine and everything is good here. So you

really have nothing yet? I thought Kenai was the best."

I huff. "He's a dick, that's what he is."

She laughs. "Well, we already knew that. I hope he comes up with something soon. Poor Kaity, she could be anywhere."

"I know," I say, hating the way my heart throbs at the sound of my sister's name.

Kenai bursts through the door, looking so damned fine I have to swallow to keep a satisfied moan from leaving my lips. He's dressed in black jeans, a dark gray shirt, and those damned sexy boots. His hair is wet, a few strands stuck to his forehead, and he's clean-shaven. I can see every outline of his masculine jaw. God, he's hot. So damned hot. *Asshole.*

"I have to go, caveman just barged in. I'll call you later."

"Stay safe, you never know who you might run into. These men could be dangerous."

"I'll be okay. See you, honey."

"Laters."

I end the call and stand up. "Ready?"

"Am I here?" he mutters, but I don't miss his eyes glide over my body. Something flares in his gaze as he looks away, jaw tight.

"Let's get this over with."

He grunts and walks towards the door, opening it and waving a hand for me to exit the room. I stride past him, flicking my hair over my shoulder as I go. He makes a frustrated sound, but follows me downstairs. We take his truck over to the club, which is already flowing with people.

"Don't talk to anyone, don't ask questions. Just sit down and shut your mouth. Hear me?"

"I hear you," I mumble.

"I mean it, Marlie. Just zip it."

"Yeah, Chief, I hear you."

He gives me a long look, then we line up to enter the club. It takes ten minutes to get in, and the second we do we're surrounded by people. I push through the crowd behind Kenai, until we reach the bar. He pulls out a stool and points to it. "Sit. I'll be back soon."

I sit my ass down, glaring at him as he waves the bartender down. "Vodka soda for her."

"How do you know what I'm drinking?"

"I heard Jeffery order it for you."

"It was Jacob, and how observant of you."

He says nothing, as always, and when my drink arrives he simply turns and disappears into the crowd. I glance around, taking in the well-loved club. It's clearly been here for a while, but it's well maintained. Wooden floors, wooden bar and stools, but everything else is red. The booths, the décor. It has a slight country feel, only there isn't one single person in here even remotely country.

In fact, most of them seem quite . . . rough.

"What're you doin' here alone, pretty girl?"

I turn towards the sound of the husky, slightly inebriated voice and see a man staring at me with a toothy grin. He's around thirty, maybe a little older, and he has messy black hair and blue eyes. He's cute. Not gorgeous, but cute. He leans against the bar, probably because he seems to be having trouble standing straight.

"Just waiting for a friend," I smile politely and glance back at my drink.

Drunk men. Ugh.

"Your friend a boy or girl?"

What a dumb question.

"A man. A big, scary man," I mutter.

"Let me buy you a drink while you wait."

I hold up my drink. "I've got one."

"I can tell you're special," he says, eyes scanning the crowd. "I come here a lot. See a lot of faces. Don't often see girls like you in here."

"Girls like me?"

"Yeah, the ones who are pretty and sweet."

"I'm neither of those things. I'm just here waiting for my friend to look for . . . his friend."

"Oh yeah, who's his friend?"

I shrug. "Don't know his name."

"Hmmmm."

I study him and wonder if he's ever seen Kaity in the area. It can't hurt to ask. Right? I pull out my phone and bring up a picture of my sister. "You haven't seen this girl by any chance, have you?"

He squints, studying the picture, and something flashes in his eyes for the briefest second. Most people wouldn't notice it, but I became really attuned to studying every little bit of body language after I escaped. Now it's something I notice right away. "Nah," he says. "Never seen her. Why?"

I put my phone away. "No reason."

"I gotta go, friend just showed," he says, pushing off the bar. "Nice to meet you, Marlie."

He disappears and my skin prickles. I didn't tell him my name. I shove off the stool and turn, studying the crowd to try to find him. When I push through them, I see him disappear into a back hall. It takes me five minutes to get past the crowd, and when I do, I rush into the hall. There are restrooms on the right and a door at the end. I go to the door and push through it.

I step out into a parking lot where three men are huddled, talking. The man who I was just talking to is one of them. I rush over, without thought, and say, "Hey!"

He stops talking and they all turn. I focus on the other two men quickly. One is short, bald, and angry-looking. The other is tall and lean, with dark hair and piercing blue eyes. Complete opposites. My eyes focus back on the man I was talking to. He's the one I need to speak with.

"Did I forget something?" he says, but there is something in his eyes . . . something . . . off.

"You called me Marlie."

"That's what you said your name is."

I shake my head. "I never said my name. Do you know something? Do you have my sister? I swear to God . . ."

The man steps forward. "What?" he says, his voice icy.

"I just want to know where she is," I say, feeling fear creeping up my spine and stiffening my body. "If you have information, I'm willing to pay for what you know."

"I have no idea what you're talking about."

"You're lying." I say carefully. "How did you know my name? I know I didn't tell you."

"Everyone knows your name, Marlie. You're the girl who escaped The Watcher. That book you wrote was everywhere."

I flinch.

All three men laugh.

"I heard," the bald one says as he steps forward, "that he liked to touch girls. Did he touch you, Marlie?"

My ears start ringing.

"I heard," the tall one says, "that he liked to rip the girls' hair out. Did he rip your hair out, Marlie?"

My scalp prickles at the reminder.

"I heard," the first man says, laughing, "that you liked killing him. What if *you* were the monster? You're the one who murdered him, after all. What was it that happened? You stabbed him right up under his chin and into his brain?"

My knees start trembling. My vision flickers. I can't breathe.

"How did that feel, to drive a knife up into his brain?"

The sickening crunching sound that made fills my ears and I start to pant.

"What if he just needed mental help and you murdered him? Taking his life without giving him a chance to get better? Maybe the devil in the book is, indeed, you?"

Bile burns in my throat as I drop to my knees.

"Aw, looks like we've upset her, boys. I hear he had a family. I wonder how they feel right now?"

A family? Did he really have a family?

How did I never know that?

My body begins to tremble and I press my hands over my ears.

"She's supposed to be tough, but look at her—pathetic."

I rock.

"She's lost her sister. I wonder if that's because her sister's terrified to be around her. I would be. After the way she massacred that man."

"Stop," I whimper.

"Maybe your sister doesn't want to be found, Marlie. Imagine being related to someone who exploits themselves and their family after going through something like you did?"

"Stop!" I scream, launching up and throwing myself at the closest male.

A fist flies out and hits me before I make it, sending me flying backwards. I land on the ground with a thud, and my vision is swimming as I try to get back up. Pain radiates through my skull. Someone grabs my wrists, jerking me up, but I can't see who through my rapidly closing eye. God, the pain.

Suddenly I'm on the ground again and the sounds of grunting can be heard. I push up to my elbows, head pounding, to see Kenai beating the ever-loving hell out of the men. He takes them as if they're small children, not grown men. His fists fly, his big body overpowers theirs on a massive scale. One turns and runs, blood dripping from his nose.

He knocks the other two out cold.

Then he's looking at me, panting, knuckles bloodied. He strides over and leans down, scooping me into his arms. I try to look at him, but my face is screaming in pain. "Focus on me and follow my finger," he says. I focus on him with my good eye. He puts his finger up, moving it left and right then up and down towards my nose. "How does it feel?" he asks, voice gruff.

"It hurts," I say, voice weak.

"Come on, we need to get ice on that."

"Kenai . . . those men . . ."

"I asked you not to talk to anyone," he says. His voice isn't harsh, and I think that hurts even more.

"I know, but . . ."

"One request, Marlie."

I close my mouth and my good eye.

Then I try really hard to stop their words from penetrating my already broken soul.

TEN

Kenai takes me back to the hotel, and the second I sit on the bed, he goes and gets some ice. I caught a glimpse in the mirror when we came in, and looked away horrified. My eye is puffy and swollen shut, but it's my broken expression that scares me. Those men, what they said . . . I just don't understand. They knew so much. So much.

"Here, hold this against your eye. I don't know that it's going to do much good now, but it'll help a little. I'll get some painkillers for you."

He moves into his room as I press the ice to my eye with a hiss. After a few minutes, it goes numb and I close my eyes. My head is pounding. Kenai comes back and drops two pills into my hand. I shove them into my mouth and swallow them with a sip of water from the bottle he hands me next.

"Kenai," I say, my voice wobbly.

He looks down, still standing in front of me. "Yeah?"

"Those men . . . knew me."

He narrows his eyes, then kneels in front of me. "How do you mean?"

"The man approached me at the bar and was talking to me, but I never gave him my name. I showed him a picture of my sister and—"

"You what?"

He sounds angry.

Shit.

"I thought he might have seen her and—"

"Jesus, Marlie. I told you not to ask questions. I asked one thing of you."

Anger explodes in my chest. "I know, okay," I yell, tossing the ice. It skitters across the floor. "I know you did, but she's *my* sister. She's the *only* thing I have left. Dammit, I can't just sit around and do nothing."

"You could have been hurt far worse tonight. I'm telling you to be quiet for a reason!"

"I know that, but I'm just . . ." My voice trails off and I look away.

"You're scared, I understand that. But I make rules for a reason, Marlie. You need to follow them."

I say nothing.

"Now tell me the rest of the story."

I take a shaky breath and continue. "After I showed him the picture, he said he had to go, and then he said my name. But I hadn't told him my name. When I went outside to confront him, he and his friends started taunting me. They said they knew about me from the book, and were saying horrible things."

"Anyone who's read the book would recognize you, Marlie."

"I've been recognized before, Kenai," I snap. "I know how they reacted, and that wasn't normal. The way they were speaking, the way they were taunting me and going on about my sister . . . I could swear they were made to do that. Like someone had put them up to saying those things to me. It wasn't just a coincidence."

"You're being paranoid," he says, more carefully.

"Don't," I warn. "One thing I've learned the hard way in life is to always trust your instincts. My instincts told me they knew more about me than just reading a book could tell them and they wanted to torment me. Why, I don't know, but I'm telling you they did."

He says nothing, and I look up to see him studying me.

"I'm not being paranoid," I say softly.

"I'll look into it, into them. I picked up a wallet, so I have one of their I.D.s. For now, you need to rest."

"Did you find anything out at the club?" I ask, watching as he goes over and picks up my ice and hands it back to me.

"Yeah, I found the guy we were looking for, someone I was told by a very good source is a close associate of Chris's. He claims to have no idea what I'm talking about and says he's never heard of a Chris or a Kaitlyn before."

"What if he's lying?"

"I have no doubt he is, but I'm not a cop. I can't just arrest him and bring him in for questioning."

"So what are you going to do?"

"I'm going to follow him," he says simply. "You're going to go to sleep."

"But—"

"Now, Marlie."

His voice is firm, but slightly gentle.

I clamp my mouth shut. "You're going tonight?"

He nods, jerking the covers back and pointing. "Into bed. Now."

His voice gets even softer when he says that, and I can see a flash of genuine concern in his eyes.

"If I didn't know better," I mumble, climbing in, "I'd say you like me, Chief."

He snorts, but I swear I see it. Something light, something sweet, even. "Go to sleep, I'll be back soon."

"What if you need protection?" I mumble sleepily.

This bed is so nice.

I swear he makes a low, wheezing sound. Like he was about to laugh. "I'll try to manage without your protection."

I laugh softly. "Thanks for having my back out there tonight."

My eyelids droop. Whatever painkillers he gave me are good.

"I'll come check on you when I get back, make sure you're still alive."

I smile. At least, I think I do.

"I knew you liked me."

He doesn't say anything and I drift off, my world going a comfortable shade of black. Before everything slips away completely, I could swear I hear him say, "Maybe I do."

I'm so hungry.

I'm so thirsty.

Mostly, I'm terrified.

So damned afraid.

He's left me in this room for an entire day since he made me hold those pieces of hair. My stomach coils tightly at the thought. I can escape this. I can. I just have to be smarter than him. I have to keep my wits about me. I can't break. I close my eyes against the horrific images of the bloodied scalps.

God, those poor girls.

The door rattles.

I jerk up in bed, my hands still tightly secured behind me. My ankles are bound as well. Fear unlike anything I've ever felt lodges in my chest as he opens the door, dragging in a television. He's got a massive knife in his hand, and a grin on his face.

"*Good evening, Marlie. How are you feeling today?*"

He's speaking to me as if I'm a patient in a hospital and he's a doctor. He's so calm, as if we're in a perfectly normal situation. I say nothing. I don't want to give him anything. Not a single damned thing.

"*I'm well, thanks for asking,*" *he continues.* "*I've been out there all day preparing this video for you. Would you like to watch it?*"

No.

Please no.

He laughs. "*Of course you do. You'll be so proud of me, Marlie. The other girls were, I'm sure.*"

I close my eyes as he plugs the television in.

"*You can close your eyes, but I assure you that I'll remove a finger every time you do. Then I'll move on to your toes. The decision is yours.*"

My eyes open and tears burn under my eyelids. He will. He'll do it. He's going to make me watch this horror, because if I don't, he'll make me suffer in the worst possible ways. Could anything truly be worse than watching him remove the scalps of innocent girls?

"*There now, smart girl. Let's begin, shall we?*"

He presses PLAY, *and the picture zooms in on a small, blonde girl sitting on a bed. She's battered, bruised, bloodied, and skinny. He's had his fun with her. He wants to end her now. Her knees are a mess, broken and shattered, skin hanging from them. She's naked, but so covered in bruises and cuts, it's hard to notice.*

My entire body coils tightly. I want to pass out. I want to die. I want something to stop this horror.

"This is Kelly," he says, sitting beside me on the bed, fingering the knife. "She fought me a lot. She just couldn't learn a lesson. Take note of her fingers? Oh wait," he laughs. "She has none."

My eyes train in on the girl's hands. They're a mess, but he's right, she has no fingers and no toes.

I'm going to be sick.

He enters the room in the video, a huge hunting knife in his hand. I'm praying for my vision to black out. I can't watch this. I can't. He walks over, taking her hair in his hands and jerking her head back. He says something to her, but the ringing in my ears blocks it out. I can't stop it, I close my eyes.

He moves like lightning, taking hold of my hand and bringing the knife to one of my fingers.

"No," I scream. "I'll watch, I'll watch!"

He lets me go, eyes burning into mine. "I won't give you a second chance," he hisses. "Now watch my perfection. My art."

I force my eyes back to the screen just as he brings the knife to the top of her scalp.

I'm screaming before he's even started cutting.

"Marlie!"

"No!" I flail around, hitting the hard body hovering over mine. "No, please."

"Marlie, stop. It's me."

"Get off me!" I scream. "Get off me. Help! Somebody please help."

"Marlie!"

Something cold hits my face and my eyes jerk open. I'm panting, covered in sweat, and there is a big body on mine, holding my hands above my head.

"It's me, hey, it was a dream."

Kenai?

A dream.

Oh God. He's holding me down because I was having a nightmare. Shame fills my body and I start thrashing again. "Let me go."

"Marlie . . ."

"Kenai, let me go."

Realizing I'm awake, he hesitantly releases me. I roll off the bed and run towards the bathroom. My knees give out halfway there, clearly having strained themselves trying to get Kenai off during my nightmare. I hit the ground, my hands slapping against the carpet. I cry out in frustration and pain.

"Shit."

"Don't," I cry, hearing Kenai's feet hit the floor. "Please, don't."

"Marlie . . ."

I force myself up, and hobble the rest of the way to the bathroom. I make it, slam the door, and then lower myself to the ground, back pressed against the wood. I can't believe he saw that. I'm so embarrassed. I clench my eyes shut, reaching up and rubbing them furiously to stop any tears that attempt to fall. Pain radiates through my face, reminding me of my very sore, very swollen eye.

Get it together.

You're okay.

You're stronger than this.

I force myself up and walk to the mirror. My face looks awful, puffy and sore. My eye is swollen shut. I wash it anyway, removing the sticky sweat from my skin. Then I take a few calming breaths and hobble back out into my room. Kenai is still standing by my bed, and his eyes find mine the second I come out.

"Sorry," I mumble to the floor.

"Look at me."

I flinch. "Kenai, it was a nightmare . . ."

"Now, Marlie."

I look up at him. "Are you okay?"

"Yeah—"

"The truth," he demands, but his voice is the softest I've ever heard it.

"No," I whisper.

"What makes them go away?"

"The dreams? Nothing."

"What have you tried?"

"Outside of knocking myself out with drugs, nothing."

He glances at my bed, then back at me. "This means nothing, understand that. It's just a proven method."

I narrow my eyes, confused.

He removes his shirt as my mouth drops open.

"I'm not sleeping with you!" I snap.

He gives me a look. "Don't flatter yourself. That's not what I'm doing."

I huff. "Then what are you doing?"

"Sleeping next to you."

"Why?"

"Because . . . it helps."

"Nice try, buddy."

He shakes his head with exasperation, turns to me—all muscle and bronze skin—strides over, launches me into his arms, and drops down onto the bed, rolling us as if I weigh nothing, so he's tucked behind me, his big body wrapped around mine.

"I'm not going to lie, this is awkward," I mumble, pretending it doesn't feel incredible to have him beside me.

"Ditto. Now go to sleep."

"You're not going to wake with morning wood are you, because that will just make things weird."

"I can't control my dick."

"Perhaps you should try. Before you go to sleep, think about something that's not sexy at all. Like your mom in a thong perhaps."

He makes a groaning sound, and his body jerks, then he mutters, "Shut up and go to sleep."

"I'm just saying . . ."

"Sleep."

"You're so bossy."

"Now," he orders.

"Does anybody actually listen to you when you order them around?"

He makes a frustrated sound. "Do you ever fucking listen to anybody when they tell you to shut the hell up and go to sleep?"

I think on that. "Absolutely not."

"Well, it's about time you learn. I have methods to make you stop talking."

"Is this about to get sexual? I knew you were attracted to me!"

"Jesus Christ woman, zip it."

"It's not *my* fault you're a perv."

"You started it," he mutters. "Now go the fuck to sleep."

"There was a book written about that . . ."

"Fuck," he barks. "Seriously, do you ever shut up?"

I smile, even though he can't see it. "Goodnight, Chief."

He grunts.

My smile gets bigger as I drift into blissful nothingness.

ELEVEN

"Hey," I say groggily into the phone, rolling away from Kenai's hard, warm body.

I can't believe I slept next to him all night.

But I had the most amazing night's sleep.

"Sorry to wake you so early, Marlie, but I got a strange phone call today."

It's Hannah, and she sounds worried.

I sit upright, waking Kenai in the process. He rolls and murmurs, "What is it?" in that sleepy, sexy male voice that they all have when they wake up in the morning.

Focus.

"Who was it? Was it about Kaity?"

"Yeah. It was a call for her, I don't know how they got my number. They were looking for her. I played along and said I hadn't seen her that day but I'd pass on a message when I did. They told me to tell her to meet them at an address."

"Where?" I say, sliding off the bed.

"In Vegas, which was strange."

"We're in Vegas. Give me the address."

"I don't know," she says hesitantly. "It doesn't sound safe. I think it's dangerous. I should call the police."

"So they can blow us off again and bungle what might be a good lead? No, Hannah. If whoever is there has contact with my sister, or might know where she is, I want to know."

She hesitates again. "Okay."

She gives me an address and makes me promise to call her. I disconnect and turn to Kenai. "Hannah got a strange phone call from a guy looking for Kaity. He wants her to go to some address here in Vegas."

Kenai narrows his eyes. "Why would anyone call Hannah?"

I shrug. "She's Kaity's best friend—if someone had Kaity's phone they'd be able to find her number and figure it out. Do you think it's a set up? Hannah thought we should involve the police, but I told her no. Do you think she was right?"

Kenai looks confused. "No. I'll figure it out. It could be what you said, but it still doesn't make sense why they'd call her. She's in Denver."

"Maybe just to see if she's in contact with Kaity?" I suggest.

He nods, looking slightly impressed. "Yeah, that

could be true. If they're looking for Kaity, they might be trying to see if Hannah knows where she is."

"Makes sense."

"We'll go check out the place, it might give us a lead."

"Did you get anything last night?" I ask, walking towards the bathroom.

"Nothing."

I stop and turn to him. "Does all of this feel a little off to you?"

I don't know why I said that, but something inside just doesn't feel quite right. It's felt like that for a few days now, and I've mostly put it down to nerves and anxiety because I want to find my sister. The truth is, it feels like something isn't adding up, but I can't put my finger on what. The gunshots. The men in the parking lot. It all seems a bit too coincidental.

"Yeah," Kenai says, standing. "I just don't know what it is. I'll figure it out. Get dressed, we'll check out this place."

I nod and disappear into the bathroom. I shower, dress, and then eat the breakfast Kenai orders. When we're done, we hit the road and make our way towards the address Hannah gave me. It leads us to an old, seemingly abandoned warehouse a fair distance off of the Strip. My heart clenches as I stare at it.

It doesn't look like anyone is here.

"I think it's empty."

"Why would they send Kaity to an abandoned warehouse?" Kenai says, rubbing his jaw and staring at the old, rusty building.

"Should we go in?"

"No one is here, so yeah."

He reaches into the glove compartment and pulls out his gun. He tucks it into his pants, and then we climb out. It makes me feel a little better to know we've got some protection. I can't see all that well because of my puffy, sore eye, so I stick close to Kenai as we move towards the warehouse. When we reach the front door, Kenai pushes it open. It creaks loudly.

Both of us stop.

Waiting. Listening.

Nothing happens, so we push in further. There is junk everywhere, from old cars to furniture, all of it covered in dust. As we move in, Kenai whispers "Be careful," as we start looking through the stuff. It doesn't look like anyone has been here for months, years even. It doesn't make any sense.

"Look around, see if you can see anything that might help us figure out why they'd want Kaity to come here."

I scan my surroundings, shoving things aside, coughing from the dust. I move towards the left end of the warehouse, and Kenai moves to the right. I find an old couch with a blanket strewn over it. I lift the blanket and gasp, a ragged cry leaving my throat as I lean down, lifting a soft, red dress into my hands.

I'd recognize that dress anywhere. I'd recognize it because I bought it for Kaity two years ago.

"Kenai," I croak, hands trembling as tears form under my eyelids.

"What is it?"

"This is hers. This dress is Kaity's."

He takes it from my hands and looks around.

"Oh God. Someone has her. I was right. Kenai . . ."

My voice is becoming frantic and I'm starting to freak out, so much so I don't realize that Kenai hasn't spoken since I handed him the dress. I look up at him and see he's studying the couch.

"We have to get out of here," he says so suddenly I'm confused.

"What?"

"Now!" he barks, taking my arm and pulling me towards the exit.

"Kenai, she could be here. She might come back. Someone might show up. We can't leave."

He keeps pulling me, and I can't dislodge him. I cry out in frustration, kicking and clawing, but he keeps pulling me until we burst out the front door.

"Kenai!" I scream.

He pulls out his gun just as a loud shot rings out. We both drop to the ground, and my words get trapped in my throat. "Move," Kenai barks as another shot rings out, hitting so close to my leg that I can't stop the scream that tears from my lips.

Kenai shoots in the direction of the gunshots, all while moving like a ninja across the ground. I try to follow, but my heart is in my throat and my body is alert with fear. More shots ring out, coming so close. God, we're going to die.

"Kenai," I cry. "What's happening?"

He twists, shoots, and then launches up, taking me with him. He swings the truck door open and throws me in. A gunshot hits the windshield, which explodes into a thousand pieces. My screams turn to frantic sobs as I'm showered in glass. Kenai manages to get around the other side and barks, "Stay down."

Then he hits the gas.

Shots keeping ringing out, hitting the car, until we're far enough away that whoever was back there can no longer see us. Only then do I lift myself up, glass shards dropping off my body.

"Don't move, Marlie. That glass is like mini razor blades and will slice into your skin without effort."

I stare down, seeing spots of blood already forming on my arms and legs.

"Wh-Wh-Wh-What just happened?" I stammer, my voice thick.

"We got set up, that's what happened."

"I don't . . . How do you know that?"

"The warehouse was rundown and shitty, yet that blanket was placed so perfectly. It was clean. The dress was clean. It was put there to be found. Someone knew we were in the area and called Hannah, clearly connecting the dots, knowing she'd give you the address. It's genius, really."

I hadn't even realized the blanket was clean. "So someone called her, knowing she'd let us know so we'd go out there and get killed?"

He nods harshly.

"Who would do that!"

"Whoever it is doesn't like that we're looking for Kaity, and they're trying to get us out of the picture."

Oh. My. God.

"Are we safe?"

He looks to me, his eyes intense. "Not anymore."

We go back to the hotel after dropping off Kenai's truck to get the windshield replaced. He spends the next two hours on the phone, while I just clutch Kaity's dress, holding it close, praying that she's okay. God, what if she's already gone? I can't bear it. I can't. I feel like this is all my fault. After everything that happened to me, she suffered and I wonder how much support she had? She deserved someone to look after her, too. If she'd had that, she might not have felt the need to get herself involved with the wrong kind of crowd.

Kenai gets annoyed at whoever is on the other end of the phone and tosses it across the room, then turns and walks to the window. It's late afternoon, and another day has passed with us getting into more trouble than actually finding anything helpful. What if we're wrong? What if we're on the complete wrong track?

"What if it isn't anything to do with her boyfriend and drugs? What if someone else has her?"

He doesn't turn. "No."

"But, it seems unlike something that drug dealers would do. It seems . . . more deranged."

He spins around, clearly still pissed at whatever happened on the phone. "Don't let your paranoia take over, Marlie. This is about finding your sister. I know it's hard, believe me, I can see it in your face, but I need you to be strong. If you can't handle it, maybe I should continue on my own."

My mouth drops open, then I get angry. "What if you're wrong? Huh?"

He takes a deep breath, trying to be patient. "I'm not wrong. I'll find who is doing this, but it has nothing to do with the man that took you, or some other crazy-ass killer. You need to stay focused on the here and now. You're letting your past come into play, and you need to stop and trust me."

"That dress was left there and—"

"Enough," he says, his voice tight. "You're wasting our time and energy, and we don't have any to spare."

Wasting our time and energy? He can't be serious? My heart clenches and for a moment, I just stare at him as I process those words over and over in my head. How dare he accuse me of wasting time and energy. How dare he. Anger bubbles in my chest. He doesn't get it. He'll never get it. I'm not doing any of this for me. This is all for Kaity.

"You know what?" I scream, unable to hold my anger back any longer. "You won't listen to me, so I'm done listening to you."

"Marlie!" he calls as I spin and turn to rush out. "Don't leave. I'm not trying to be an asshole, I'm just trying to keep emotion out of this. One of us has to think clearly."

I look at him. "You couldn't possibly understand the emotion, Kenai. You can't ask me to take it out, because you don't understand it."

"No," he says, his eyes softening a little. "I don't understand it. I just know my job, and what I have to do. I'm not saying you're wrong, I'm not saying you're not right to feel the things you feel. I'm simply telling you we need to focus on what is happening now, and not on what happened in the past."

My anger still bubbles in my chest, and I cross my arms, trying not to let it explode out of me further. I wish he could understand where I'm coming from. I wish he could see it from my side. I know he's trying to do his job, but it's like he is refusing to see anything that I'm saying. Refusing to look. "I've learned to trust my instincts, my gut, my feelings, more than anything. Something is off . . ."

"Maybe, but you hired me. It's my job to figure that out. Not yours."

"Then you shouldn't have brought me!" I say, rushing out of the room.

He calls after me, but I don't stop. I just need to

breathe. I take the elevator to the roof and thankfully no one is up here. I walk over to the brick edge and throw my legs over, sitting on it, feet dangling over the side. Maybe he doesn't understand me because I've never told him. I never really tell anyone. The book, it was a recap of something that wasn't really through my eyes, but through stories created by my mother and the police and the media. I've never really just sat and told anyone what really happened. How it really felt.

"Get down."

I hear Kenai's voice behind, but I don't turn. I just stare out over the tall buildings.

"Marlie . . ."

"I helped him when he dropped his briefcase," I say softly. "He dropped it and I walked over and helped him. Just like that. For being a good person I ended up in the hands of a killer."

"Marlie, get down."

I keep talking.

"I don't know where he took me, but I do remember how chipper he was. He was always happy and chirpy, like he was doing nothing wrong. The first day I was there he made me hold one of the girls' scalp. He just threw it at me. I couldn't get it off."

My voice breaks, but I keep talking. He wants to judge and dismiss me, he can judge and dismiss the whole story and not just his version, or the media's version, or anyone else's version but my own. When he's heard that, then he can judge me.

"The next day he made me watch a video of one of the girls being scalped. It was the most horrific thing I've ever seen in my entire life. I can't sleep a single night without those images in my head."

Kenai is quiet now, so I keep going. I don't know if he's still behind me, I don't really care.

"He said he'd cut my fingers off if I didn't watch. The girl in the video, she had no fingers and she had no toes. He used to make me brush their hair. Hair that was no longer attached to heads."

I laugh bitterly.

"I escaped, tricked him and got out. You know what I did? I ran into the damned closet. That was, without a doubt, the dumbest moment of my life. That's when he broke my knees. Just smashed them with a baseball bat."

Kenai makes a throaty sound, letting me know he's still there. He sounds pained.

"I escaped the second time because he didn't give me a strong enough dose. I managed to get away. I dragged my body into the kitchen and got a knife. He came over the counter, ripped my hair clean out of my head. I still have bald spots. I killed him. Somehow, I drove that knife up into his brain from under his chin. That image and sound haunt me the most."

"Marlie," Kenai says, his voice thick.

"You think you know me—you know nothing. You can't even begin to imagine how it felt to get home after that. Everyone wanted something from me. Police, reporters, publishers, the other girls' families, my own family. They wanted so much and yet I couldn't even function. I don't remember a single thing about those first few months. I was numb. Dead. I might have been functioning, but I wasn't there."

I take a deep shaky breath.

"My mom wrote the book, released it under my name, the one you've been judging me for since the moment we met. Suddenly I was famous overnight. I didn't stop her. I barely had the strength to get through each day, I was so broken. I didn't know what was happening, I really didn't care. My mother is selfish like that. Instead of being there for me, she made millions out of my story. Since she wrote it under my name I got all the money, but she guilts me into giving it to her. She could take it all, but I guess she's not *that* greedy. I don't ever touch that money and will never. I used some to pay you to help me find my sister. Otherwise, I live in a shitty shack in Colorado Springs and drive a rundown truck, because I want no part in it."

"Marlie . . ."

"So next time you think you know me, guess again." My voice hardens. "And don't be so quick to brush aside my instincts. If I hadn't followed them before, we wouldn't be here now."

A hand curls around my shoulder and I flinch.

"Get down," he says, but his voice is softer than I've ever heard it.

I swing my legs around and slide off, looking up at him. "I can take your anger, your bossy attitude, everything. But I can't take you judging me any longer. I don't deserve it. You can't even begin to imagine how it feels to walk in my shoes."

"I'm sorry."

I blink. "Pardon?"

"I'm fuckin' sorry. You're right, I judged without knowledge, and for that, I'm sorry. I just told you to disregard your past, but if I was being honest, it's my own past that made me judge you. And that was wrong."

"Your past?" I say softly.

"I'm not ready to talk about it," he adds, carefully, "but believe me when I say I understand how it feels to read things wrong, or to be misjudged. My past created the man I am today, it made me the tracker I am, and I know your past made you who you are. I respect that, but I need you to trust me, Marlie. I can promise you that I'm doing everything in my power to bring your sister home safely."

Well then. I didn't expect that.

He reaches down, cupping my jaw. "I've met a lot of people in my life, Marlie, but I've never met one as strong as you are."

My heart flutters and tears burn under my eyelids.

"You're incredible."

Oh God.

Then he leans down and his mouth brushes

against mine. It's so light I wonder if I've imagined it, but his hand is on my cheek and his body is so close to mine we're nearly pressed together, so I know I'm not imagining it. Screw it. I reach up, curling my fingers around his neck and bring him closer, slamming his lips against mine.

He groans.

I moan. It's been so long since I've felt this way.

And then he kisses me like he means it, parting his lips, letting his tongue slide into my mouth. I gasp and take it, pressing myself closer to him, tugging his hair and relishing in his throaty rasp. We kiss deep, and we kiss long. Only when a throat clears behind us, do we pull apart. A family, two adults and two kids, stand on the rooftop, looking embarrassed.

"Sorry," the father says. "We were just going to watch the sun go down."

"No problem," Kenai says, his voice thick. "We were just leaving."

Kenai takes my hand and leads me off the rooftop.

But it doesn't escape my notice that he doesn't look at me.

Not once.

TWELVE

Kenai avoids me when we get back to the hotel room. In fact, he doesn't say another word, just climbs into his bed and rolls to his side. He regrets the kiss, I know he does. I understand why he would—after all he's a serious man and his job is everything. He probably just crossed every line he'd ever laid out for himself.

But it was an amazing kiss. There was something there, a feeling, a stir of emotions, I'm sure of it.

Or maybe he just felt sorry for me.

With a sigh, I climb into my own bed. He didn't offer for me to sleep with him tonight, understandably, so I guess I'm cutting this one on my own. I lay down and put a hand over my eyes, inhaling deeply and trying to stop the flurry of memories that are swirling around in my brain.

Talking about it was good, but it also brought them all to the surface and that's going to make sleeping difficult.

Still, somehow I manage to drift off into a somewhat restless sleep.

"You've been such a good girl today, Marlie. I have a surprise for you."

I look up from the bed. I'm so hungry my stomach feels like it's twisting in on itself. I'm thirsty. I'm tired. I can't sleep because every single time I close my eyes, I see him scalping those girls. The blood. The screams. Vomit rises in my throat but I can't put a hand up to press against my mouth to stop it from rising any further. It doesn't matter. There's nothing in my body left to come out.

My eyes find him in the doorway. He's got . . . oh God. Bile burns my throat and I turn my head away, unable to look. He's got all the scalps, with the long hair flowing off them. My fingers tremble and my body starts to shake as he comes in closer, tossing them on the bed.

"I've just washed their hair, my favorite time of the week. I've got one in every color. Don't you think they're beautiful? I think they'd look a lot nicer if you did them."

Oh God.

No.

He can't make me do that.

"I don't need to explain what'll happen if you disobey me. You don't want that, do you, Marlie? You've been such a good little helper these last few

days. I might just let you live a little longer, as a reward. Try out some new games. What do you think?"

I want to die. That's what I think.

But I can't. I won't. He will not beat me. He will not hurt me.

I'll do whatever he wants if it gives me one more day to have the chance to escape this place.

I look towards the hair. He's got red ribbons with little white polka dots tied around the ponytails. I swallow my bile. Switch off. Just do what he asks and turn it off.

"I'd like them braided," he says in a singsong voice as he uncuffs me.

I could fight him, but I know right now I'm not strong enough and I can see the bulge from the knife and gun he's got tucked into his pants. I'd barely make it out the door. He steps back once I'm uncuffed and pulls out his gun, training it on me. "You know the rules, every time you do something wrong, I'll shoot."

I swallow, and with trembling fingers and aching wrists I pick up the brush he's set down and the first lock of hair. Tears burn under my eyelids as I run the brush through it. I can't do this. I can't. Oh God. My hands start rattling, but he seems oblivious.

"That was Sasha. She tried to provide me with sexual favors for her release," he snorts and shakes his head. "She should know that sexual favors don't work on me. I don't need them."

The hair is long and a soft, honey brown. God. I want to die.

"Brush it, Marlie."

I keep brushing it, keeping my hands away from the scalp. I can't touch that. I won't touch that.

"Pretend Sasha is here, pretend you're having a little girls party. What would you say to her?"

Sick.

He's so fucking sick.

"I-I-I'd say—"

"Don't talk to me, Marlie, talk to Sasha."

Deranged.

Sick.

"Are you still seeing that boy, Sasha?" I croak out.

Keep the tears in.

"Very good," he sings. "What would Sasha say back?"

"I am, M-M-Marlie, he's so good-looking don't you think?"

He shifts and I don't miss the bulge in his pants as he watches the exchange with lusty eyes. This gets him off. The sick fuck.

"Keep going," he rasps, sliding the knife out and running his fingers over the blade.

"I do think so," I whisper. "I think he's very handsome."

"Make her tell you what she's going to do with him," he demands, fingering the knife so hard that blood appears on his fingers.

No.

I can't.

I can't do this.

"Marlie!"

I jerk awake and sit up, hands going to my hair. It's there. It's still there. I'm panting and covered in a cold sweat. It's dark. I can't see anything, but I can hear Kenai's voice, strong and steady, bringing me out of my haze. I can't stop the tears that burst forth and run down my face, or the strangled sob that leaves my throat.

"Hey," he says, his voice still slightly husky from sleep. "Hey, it's okay. It was just a dream."

I sob harder, wrapping my knees up to my chest and hanging on tightly.

"Dammit," he murmurs, and then I feel his hard body come closer to mine before his arms go around me and pull me close.

I sob harder.

"One day, you'll sleep peacefully. One day, I promise you, you won't wake up to the horror of him," Kenai says, his voice gentle.

"I don't believe that." I hiccup. "I feel like I'll never stop seeing those images."

"Maybe it won't be every night, maybe at times they'll appear, but I promise you there will come a time it'll get easier."

His hand strokes down my hair, and it feels so incredibly good to be comforted. "Kenai?" I whisper through my sobs.

"Yeah?"

"Will I ever be normal again?"

"No," he says honestly.

His words scare me. For a moment, panic rises in my chest and my heart starts pounding. His answer was honest and straightforward, said without even a pause. Like he knows. Like he can see something I can't. Am I that obvious? Do people really just look at me and know, deep down in their souls, that I'm damaged goods? Before I can think too much more, Kenai continues.

"But there is nothing wrong with that. What's normal anyway? Everyone has some kind of demon, Marlie. Some worse than others. Normal isn't reality. This is you now. It doesn't make you weaker, or stronger, it's just the new version. Accept it. Make it the best you can. Then, at the very least, you can say it didn't defeat you."

I wrap my arms around his middle and hold him as tightly as I can, needing his comfort. His body is hard, he smells amazing, his skin is warm. He holds me until I calm down, his fingers gliding through my hair until my eyes get heavy, and just before I drift off, his lips brush across my forehead. "I wouldn't want you any other way. You're a brave girl, Marlie. The bravest I know."

I don't know when I fall asleep, all I know is that when I wake in the morning, I'm still in his arms. They're wrapped around me tightly, holding me secure. I feel safe for the first time since I can remember. My eyelids flutter open, and I look over to him, to see that he's staring at the ceiling, eyes open.

"Hi," I whisper. "Sorry about last night."

"Don't be sorry," he says, releasing me and shuffling out of the bed. I miss his arms the moment they're gone.

"Thank you . . . for the comfort. I needed it."

His eyes hold mine, and something travels past the hardness I carry around and delves right into my heart.

"You're welcome."

"So," I whisper. "What happens today?"

"Today we go to Los Angeles. It's time to finish this."

Why does it feel like it's not going to be that easy?

Kenai orders breakfast for us while I shower.

I take my time washing and drying my hair. I don't know why I care, but I feel the need to look good, and that's what I'm going to do. I dress once I'm done and make my way back out to the living area where he's standing, on the phone. He doesn't hear me come in, so for a moment, I just watch him.

Pure male perfection.

He hangs up and turns around, his eyes dropping to my hair, which is flowing around my shoulders. His jaw tightens and his eyes flicker away. Disappointment slams into my chest, but I force it back. I'm not here to find a relationship, I'm here to find my sister. Guilt swarms my chest and I cross my arms, suddenly feeling stupid. I shouldn't even be focusing on any of this. It shouldn't even cross my mind right now, but it's been so long since I've felt anything but fear and loneliness.

A knock sounds at the door and Kenai walks over, body stiff. He opens it, pokes his head out and looks left and right, then leans down and picks up a box. He studies the box, turning around and walking back in, kicking the door shut behind him. The package in his hands is small and poorly wrapped.

"What's that?" I ask, walking over.

He shrugs and carefully lifts it to his ear, listening.

"Do you think it's a bomb?" I squeak, taking two steps back.

He puts a finger up to his lips and listens, scowling at me. I zip it and let him do his thing. A second later, he lowers the box and rips the top off. He stares at the contents for a few seconds, before his eyes flicker to me. He's not wearing his scowl anymore, but a sympathetic expression that makes my blood run cold. "What is it?" I whisper, taking a hesitant step forward.

"Marlie . . . I think it's—"

"What?" I say, cutting him off. "Kenai, what is it?"

He sighs and hands the box to me. I take it and look down. Inside is a shirt. I recognize it instantly. It's Kaity's shirt. Her favorite. A little white top that zips up all the way from the bottom to the top at the front. It's gorgeous, and sexy, and she loved it. My fingers tremble as I lift it up and turn it over. I gasp, dropping it back in. It's covered in blood.

"Kenai," I cry, dropping the box. "That's her shirt. It's bloodied. Oh God. Oh my God."

"Marlie, take a breath," he encourages, walking over and closing his fingers around my shoulders. "Breathe."

"I can't," I cry, my chest clenching with every passing second. "Someone has her. Someone has hurt her. It's him. I know it is. I can feel it in my bones. He's setting us up. He's alive. He's   "

"Marlie, stop!" Kenai yells, forcing me to snap out of my panic enough to focus on him. "You and I both know you killed that man. Nobody can survive a knife into the brain."

"Then it's someone else or maybe someone is getting revenge for what I did. I know it doesn't make sense, but something inside me is screaming at me that I'm right. They've got my sister, they're going to . . ."

"Marlie," he says, shaking me a little. "Anyone could have sent that. If she's tied up with drugs, it could be a warning to us. You need to calm down and stay focused."

With shaky legs, I sit on the closest chair and nod. My stomach is twisting, my throat is burning, and my head is spinning. Something doesn't feel right. I feel it right down to my core, but Kenai is right—I need to stay calm. I drop my head into my hands and take a few deep breaths as he studies the box again.

"There's no note," he murmurs, more to himself than me. "Someone is just letting us know they've got her, but they're not making demands. They're also following us, because they know we're here."

I tremble.

It isn't related to drugs, I know it, but I say nothing.

"What do we do?" I ask. "Do we stay? Figure out who sent it?"

"No," Kenai says. "We keep moving. We need to find this Chris now more than ever."

THIRTEEN

Kenai and I continue our journey to Los Angeles. He's got leads and information on this Chris guy and is hoping it'll be enough to get us what we need to find Kaity. He isn't giving me much, in regards to what he's found out, but he is keeping me in the loop enough that I have a basic idea of what's going on. So far, it seems like we're being led around in circles. I know I need to trust in Kenai, and know he's good at his job, but something is not sitting well with me and it's starting to bother me.

"Why are you squirming?" Kenai asks when we're about an hour out of Los Angeles.

"I can't help it, I'm restless," I say, tucking my legs beneath me.

"You've been shifting and sighing this whole trip, Marlie. Why?"

"I think you're wrong about this not being connected to what happened to me and I wish you'd listen."

His fingers tighten around the steering wheel. "I am listening to you, I'm taking what you're saying in, but you need to trust me."

I exhale loudly. "But you're not telling me anything. You're making me try to piece it together on my own."

He sighs. "Marlie, I know you want me to tell you everything, but I'm not going to. That's my rule. You have to believe I'm doing my best. If I tell you, then you're going to freak out and start trying to sort it out on your own. That'll only make things harder. Let me do my job."

"But—" I try.

He looks away and doesn't say anything, just stares out the windshield. This conversation is over.

I sit quietly for a bit, but the awkward silence between us grows and makes me uncomfortable. Someone needs to address the elephant in the room. It's making us both tense.

"Kenai, about that kiss," I say, regretting it almost instantly when he flinches.

"It shouldn't have happened, Marlie. I'm here to do a job, and getting tangled up like that . . . it can't happen."

Right.

Shame hits me like a punch to the gut.

"Well, if you didn't want to do it, why did

you?" I snap, covering my embarrassment with anger.

"Because you were broken, and you needed to know that you weren't alone."

"So it was a pity kiss? And everything you told me last night was out of pity?" I yell, throwing my hands up, pissed that I even brought it up. "Wow. I've been a lot of things in my life, done a lot of things, but I've never been kissed out of pity."

"I didn't—" he begins, but I cut him off by throwing a hand up.

"No, don't bother. It meant nothing anyway."

The car falls silent for a few minutes, before he curses under his breath.

"What was that?" I growl, crossing my arms.

He just shakes his head.

"Fine, shut down again," I huff, turning and staring out the window. "But I'm not the only one in this car who's broken."

The rest of the drive is silent. We arrive in Los Angeles midafternoon, and Kenai immediately stops at a hotel to get us a room. I sit in his truck, staring out the window, refusing to move. He comes back out once he's checked us in and taps on the window. I look over and see him dangling the keys. I guess that means we're going up there before we go hunt down this Chris guy.

Fine by me.

I climb out of the truck and breeze past him. He mutters something along the lines of "stubborn ass woman" before following me into the hotel lobby. My phone rings just as we hit the elevator, and I glance down to see it's my mother. I'm not in the mood to chat, but I pick up in case she's worried about her daughter's safety.

"Mother," I say, pressing the phone to my ear.

"Great news, sweetheart. A film producer has expressed interest in your book being turned into a movie."

I flinch.

My body goes still and I rasp, "I beg your pardon."

Kenai turns to watch me, his eyes narrowing as he hones in on the conversation.

"Isn't it wonderful? You should see the money they're going to pay, and they said they'd keep it as true to the story as possible. This is our chance. This is it, Marlie."

I can't be hearing her right.

Something odd swells in my chest, an anger I've pushed down for so long. An anger I've ignored. An anger I should have unleashed on her so long ago. I think of my sister, sitting somewhere, terrified and alone, and all this woman is thinking about is money. No. No longer. Something explodes in my chest. Something I haven't felt for such a long, long time.

Strength.

"Marlie?" she calls.

"No," I say, my voice scratchy with emotion.

"Pardon me?"

"I said no, Mother. No. I don't accept. I do not

give you permission to do that. It's my story. You already dragged me into the spotlight with the book when what I needed was time and support to heal. I won't let you do it again. No."

"But I've already told them you would and—"

"Then un-tell them!" I scream so loudly Kenai flinches. "This is *my* life. This is *my* horror. You did not live it. You do not get to run around seeking fame from my despair. I suffered. Me. Not you. I've lived through enough, and you will not do this. If you do, I'll take every cent that's rightfully mine and remove your access to it."

She stammers on the other end of the phone.

"And if you weren't so damned selfish, you would have asked about your missing daughter, who you haven't asked about once in the last week."

"I trust that the police are taking care of it," she stammers. "Stop being so damned selfish."

I hang up the phone and launch it across the small space. It hits the mirror on the other side and bounces off. Kenai catches it in one hand, with little to no effort. Of course he does.

"Marlie," he says, his voice careful, steady.

"She wants to make a movie," I yell, grabbing my hair with both of my hands. "She wants to make more money out of my ordeal. She doesn't care. She's so damned selfish. She hasn't once asked about Kaity, or me, or any of this. It's all money, money, money."

"Marlie . . ."

"Dammit, why am I not enough?" My knees

buckle and Kenai steps closer, wrapping his arm around my waist and hauling me up. "Why am I not enough?" I whisper into his shirt. "I'm her daughter. I went through hell. Why can't she just give me what I need?"

"What do you need?" he says softly.

"I need her to care. I need her to understand. I need her to see that she's hurting me doing what she's doing."

He holds me close, and the elevator pings as we reach our floor. He guides me out and towards our hotel room. I cling on to him, tears running down my cheeks, as he uses the card to unlock the door. When we're inside, he moves us to the massive bed and we sit down.

"You have the right to say no. You have the right to refuse all of it."

I put my face in my hands. "I know I do, but I was so weak and so fragile that I had no power."

"You have power now. You have all the power to re-create your life again."

I swallow and nod, keeping my head down.

"You need some rest. Stay here. I'll go and find Chris."

"No." I jerk my head up. "Please, Kenai, I don't want to be here. I need to help. I need to know I'm doing something good."

He studies me. "Okay, but you know the rules, Marlie. Now more than ever, it's crucial you follow them."

I nod. "I won't say a word. Thank you."

He nods, then hands me my phone. "You have the power to control your life now. Don't be afraid to use it. I'm proud of you."

With that he walks into the bathroom.

I can't move.

Something explodes in my chest.

Something unfamiliar.

He told me he's proud of me.

I didn't realize until this very moment how much I needed to hear that.

The club we go to is packed. I can tell from the massive line to get in that we are waiting in.

It's just past nine and Kenai and I are wearing fancy clothes to fit into this place. My dress is short, black, and probably worth more than I make in a week at work. It's gorgeous, though. A low dip at the front, a beautiful zip up back. Kenai is wearing a suit, and God, it makes him look incredible. It fits him like a glove, hanging on to every muscle and dip of his body.

We have to dress like this, because this place is so flashy. It's expensive. It's also seedy. The people scream money and wealth, but there is an undercurrent of illegal money and high-class crime that you can feel radiating from just below the surface.

"This place is sketchy," I whisper to Kenai as we line up.

"You feel that too, huh?"

"Everyone looks like they're rich and important, but somehow you just know it isn't legit."

Kenai nods. "Yeah, I looked into this place. Man that runs it is as dirty as they come. I have an inclination he runs an underground fighting ring."

"God, they still do that?" I ask, stepping closer to him.

"Yeah, they still do that."

"So what does this Chris guy look like?"

Kenai's eyes scan the crowd. "Tall, blond, scar on his eyebrow that's quite prominent."

"Okay," I say, shifting nervously.

"Stop fidgeting," Kenai says without looking at me. "Just act normal."

"That's a bit hard when there are people staring at me."

"They're staring at you because you look fucking beautiful. Own it."

My cheeks flush as I look over at him. He's still staring straight ahead.

"Did you just give me a compliment?"

He jerks his head in a nod.

"You can't even look at me when you do it. Is it really that hard to say, even if it's a lie?" I say softly.

His head whips around, and his eyes find mine. Then he steps forward, catching me around the waist and hauling me close. My breath catches in my lungs as his lips drop down and his breath tickles my ear. In a low, seductive voice, he says, "It wasn't a lie. You're the most beautiful woman

I've ever had the pleasure of laying my eyes on, Marlie. So fucking perfect."

Then he lets me go and I take a wobbly step back.

My heart slams against my rib cage and my cheeks heat with the remembrance of his words. The line moves fast after that, probably because I keep replaying it over and over in my head. Does he really think those things, or does he just know I'm struggling with the way I am after my ordeal, so he's being kind, giving me the boost I need?

"Stop overanalyzing what I said," he murmurs when we get to the bouncer at the door. "I meant every word."

I look over to him and he's giving me an expression that tells me not to bother arguing. I don't. I'll take it. God knows I need the support. I need to feel like I'm still worth it, after everything.

We show our I.D.s and enter the club. It's gorgeous, decked out in light blues and whites. The bar is clear glass. It has a cool, calm, and elegant feel. People are standing, talking and interacting, but there is no dancing, no grinding, no games, nothing like a normal club. It almost feels like a business function of some sort.

"I'm going to start looking for Chris. Sit at the bar, and don't move," Kenai orders, leading me to the bar.

"Can't I come? I won't say anything."

"No."

He gives me a firm look, but desperation floods my chest. "She's my sister, Kenai. I know her better than anyone. Please. I won't say anything, but I might be able to help."

"Not negotiable, Marlie. I'm not putting you in danger, and if he recognizes you, he might refuse to talk."

I swallow, push it down, and nod. He has a point, and I promised I wouldn't interfere.

"Thank you," he murmurs, appreciatively.

He orders me a drink, then disappears into the crowd. I sit, sipping it and staring around. I don't notice him at first, because he's in amongst a group of people right near the back of the club, but when he turns, I can't help but notice the prominent scar that runs through his eyebrow, which fits the description Kenai gave me of Chris. He's standing, holding a glass of whiskey. His hair is slicked back and he's wearing a flashy suit. But there's a very good chance it's him. I finish my drink and stand, looking around for Kenai. He's nowhere to be seen. I move around the club, keeping my eyes on Chris but looking for Kenai.

I can't find him.

Chris and another man open a door that leads outside and disappear out of it. My heart pounds as I look around frantically for Kenai. If Chris gets away, we might never find Kaity. Does he know who Kenai is? Is he already spooked? I don't think, I just act. I rush towards the back door and burst out of it.

Chris and the other man are just exchanging a little brown packet. When they hear me, both turn. Chris studies me and his eyes widen. My sister and I share a strong resemblance, and I'm sure he knows who I am. I can see it written all over his face, which confirms that the man in front of me is Chris. But it also confirms that I'm now in danger. Shit. The other man just turns and disappears. He clearly got whatever he came for. My heart slams against my chest as I stare at the man in front of me.

The monster.

The person who ruined my sister's life.

"Marlie," Chris says, stepping forward.

"Where is she?" I hiss.

His brows shoot up. "I beg your pardon?"

"Where's Kaitlyn?"

He shakes his head and smirks. "Probably dead in an alley with some man between her legs."

Anger bubbles in my chest and I lunge forward. "Where is she? You sick son of a bitch."

He steps backwards, face scrunching with rage. "What the fuck are you going on about? I haven't seen Kaitlyn for weeks."

"Bullshit!" I yell, clenching my fists. "I know she's with you. I know she is. What have you done with her?"

He shakes his head, taking another step back. "You're fucking whacked. I haven't seen your damned sister."

"Marlie!"

Kenai's voice comes like a whip from behind me. My hands shake as I turn around and face him. He's storming towards us, anger flooding his features. He takes me by the arm and jerks me to his side. Then his eyes find Chris.

"I've been looking for you."

"Kenai Michelson." Chris grins. "How'd she afford you? Does she suck dick as good as her sister?"

Kenai flinches and steps forward, grabbing Chris by the collar and hauling him closer as if he weighs nothing. "You tell me where Kaitlyn is or I swear to fuck"—he gets right in his face—"I'll make you wish you were never born."

Chris pales a little. "Like I told your girlfriend here, I haven't seen her for weeks. She disappeared on me; figured she found someone else."

Kenai studies him. "You're a fucking liar."

"I haven't seen her," Chris snarls, shoving Kenai's chest to no avail.

"I have it on good authority you have seen her."

"Whoever told you that is a liar. I didn't even like the bitch, I was just fucking her. Wasn't even worth that. Terrible lay."

Kenai's fist flies back and he hits Chris so hard a loud crack radiates through the night. I press a hand to my mouth to stop my scream, and tears well in my eyes. Chris bellows and Kenai drops him on the ground, driving a boot into his ribs before reaching down and hauling him back up, slamming him against the wall.

"Where is she?"

"I haven't fucking seen her, you goddamned lunatic."

"She's been missing. We have multiple sources who say she's with you."

"She's not with me," Chris bellows as blood runs down his face. "That bitch isn't worth five minutes of my time."

"Then where the fuck is she?" Kenai roars into his face.

"Last time I saw Kaity she was looking at leaving because of her." He jerks a finger in my direction, and my chest clenches. "She couldn't take the entire town constantly talking about her goddamned sister, so she wanted to leave. She wanted to be free of it. So if you want to ask anyone, ask that bitch where she is. She's the reason her sister ran. Ever think she doesn't want to be found?"

My knees start to shake. Is he right? Is Kaity running because of me?

"Kaitlyn might have been struggling, but not one single person has heard from her. I don't believe she's just hiding," Kenai hisses.

"Then you're following the wrong fucking trail coming to me. I haven't seen her, and don't intend to."

"Then where the hell is she?" Kenai roars.

"I don't know!" Chris roars back.

Kenai lets him go and he leans forward, coughing a few times.

"Get the hell out of here before I put a bullet in you," Kenai growls.

"What?" I cry, rushing forward, but Kenai's arm goes out, catching me around the waist and stopping me.

"When you find the bitch," Chris growls, swiping the blood from his face with the back of his hand, "tell her she owes me fucking money."

Then he disappears inside.

"You're letting him go!" I cry, squirming in Kenai's arms.

"He's telling the truth, Marlie," he says, his voice still hard and laced with anger.

"What if he's lying? Dammit, he was our only chance."

Kenai spins me around and forces me to face him. When he speaks, his voice is surprisingly gentle. "Marlie, calm down and listen to me."

"You just let him walk away, Kenai," I cry, slapping his chest with my hands. "She could be out there, scared and alone, and you just let him go."

"He's not lying," he says, taking my shoulders in his hands and looking into my eyes.

"How do you know?" I say.

"It's my job to know. He doesn't know where she is."

"He could be a good liar. You're relying on your intuition to know if my sister is in his horrible little hands or not. We should have held him for the cops, let them check him out instead of just taking him at his word."

"Stop fighting me for a second and think about it. Stop letting your emotions get in the way. Do you truly believe he has her? Because if not, continuing to pursue him would be an incredible waste of everyone's time, and we don't have time to spare."

I stop fighting and look up at him.

"You've felt off about this from the start, and so have I."

My skin starts crawling.

"He doesn't have her, Marlie."

"Y-Y-Y-You don't know that."

He reaches down and cups my cheek. "I do know that."

My bottom lip trembles. "Then where is she?"

He shakes his head. "I don't know, but I'm going to find out."

"It's him, isn't it? The Watcher. This is somehow linked to him and—"

"Hey," Kenai says, stopping me mid-sentence. "No. I never said that. Just because it isn't Chris doesn't mean it isn't something involved in his world and the problems Kaitlyn tangled herself up in before she left."

"It's never been about drugs, I just know, Kenai . . . it's to do with *him*."

"You're freaking out, which is understandable, but you need to trust that I'll find out who it is. And don't jump to any kind of conclusions. Can you do that for me?"

I nod. "Yes, but on one condition."

"What?"

"You tell me everything you know."

His jaw twitches, and for a moment I think he's going to deny me. Then he nods once, and begins to lay out the facts.

FOURTEEN

"Where are we going?" I ask Kenai as we head to the freeway out of LA.

"We need breathing room, time to get our heads together and look back over this case. We're both tired. We're both confused. I'm sick of being in the city. So I booked us a cabin in the woods."

"In the woods?" I ask, blinking.

He nods. "Easer to stay anonymous. And I'm tired of traffic. Need to clear my head and look at this case with fresh eyes."

He makes a good point, and I won't lie and say I'm not excited to be back in nature. I miss my little house in Colorado Springs. I miss the quiet. I miss the peace. I miss just being left alone.

"Sounds good to me," I say softly, tucking my knees up to my chest.

"We'll find her, Marlie. I give you my word."

I nod, but my throat is too tight to answer. Kenai doesn't say any more, but he does reach over and take my hand, squeezing it tightly in his big one. I'm so grateful in that moment, not realizing just how much I need some type of comfort. It's been so long since I've allowed comfort in my life. I forgot just how good it feels, to know someone is there for you, that they'll support you. A simple squeeze of his hand has my chest easing just slightly.

We drive in silence, him holding my hand the entire time. We get out of town, head back towards Las Vegas, and eventually turn onto a dirt road and follow it down a few miles before arriving at a gorgeous little cabin, surrounded by thick trees and absolutely no people. I sigh with relief and climb out of the car, breathing in the fresh air. I don't even know what state I'm in but I'm already breathing a sigh of relief.

"Oh. This is perfect."

"It's nice, isn't it?" Kenai murmurs, looking around.

"Did you rent it for the night?"

"It belongs to a friend of mine. He said we could stay as long as we needed."

"That's a good friend," I say, walking towards the little cabin.

It's beautiful, set amongst the trees and patches of wildflowers. When I step up onto the porch a rustle to my left catches my attention, but when I look nothing is there. Probably some crazy wood-land animal. I smile for the first time in days and push the door open. The interior of the cabin is perfect, rustic and well taken care of. It's all mostly an open plan, with the kitchen and living areas blending into one. The furniture is warm and comfortable and there are beautiful rugs thrown down on the floor.

"This is amazing," I say as I walk in and take in the place.

"Yeah," Kenai says, coming up behind me. I can feel the brush of his body against mine as he moves past with our bags.

"Hey, Kenai?" I ask when he puts them down.

"Yeah?"

"Whoever is doing this, they're smart. So smart."

He looks to me. "Yeah, they are. But we are smarter, Marlie. I promise you we'll get to the bottom of this. Together."

Together.

My heart warms. He's letting me in. Against all his rules and regulations, he's letting me in because he respects me.

"Do you trust me?" I ask.

He looks confused for a second, then nods. "Of course I do. I don't divulge this kind of information to anyone. I respect the hell out of you."

My heart gets warmer.

"I can't stop thinking about it, you know? It goes over and over in my mind, and I try really hard to figure out what we're missing."

"We will figure it out," he says, crossing his

arms—not in a defensive way, but instead in a comfortable way.

"What if we don't?"

"Don't start doubting now, you have to stick by me with this one. We're going to work this out. We know it's not Chris, we know it's most likely been set up to look like that, we know we're on the right path now. We will find whoever is doing this, and we will get your sister back."

He's so confident in himself, in his skills, in our skills, but I just can't wrap my head around it.

"You know what I find helps," he says, walking over and taking my hand, pulling me to the sofa and sitting us both down.

"What's that?"

"Laying out what we know."

I swallow, shift a little, and nod. "Okay."

"So what do we know, Marlie?"

I'm confused for a second, wondering what it is exactly he wants me to say? Does he want me to tell him that my sister is missing and it seems we're no closer to finding out what happened to her? Or does he want me to go detective and tell him what I think?

"I'm not sure what you're asking," I admit.

"I want you to just tell me the facts. Exactly what we know about this entire case so far."

Oh. Right. I take a deep breath. "You want me to list it all?"

He nods, eyes holding mine. "Lay out the facts.

Say them out loud. It'll ease the pressure going on inside your mind and it'll make it clearer."

"Okay," I say softly. "We know Chris doesn't have Kaitlyn,"

"Before that, Marlie," he encourages.

Before that. God. Going back before that hurts. It hurts because thinking of Kaity, and thinking of all the time we've spent looking for her, makes my heart ache. But I do as Kenai asks, I answer the question.

"We know we've seemingly been led on a road trip to look for a man, that, by the sounds of it, has been set up to look like the problem."

Kenai nods.

"And you believe Chris is telling the truth, that he honestly doesn't have Kaity."

Kenai nods again.

"Which means someone else does," I say and my chest clenches. "And that person wanted us to believe that he had Kaity, and send us on a road trip for . . . what?"

"You tell me," he urges.

My mind spins with thoughts. There are so many theories, so many things I've thought, so many times I've gone back to my own situation and wondered if it all ties in. But I decide to stick with the first thing that pops into my mind, because honestly, it seems like the most logical answer. And possibly the right one.

"To distract us?"

"Why do you think someone would want to distract us?"

My stomach twists at that thought. Why would someone want to distract us? To get us away? To have longer with Kaity? To torment her more?

"I don't want to even think about it," I whisper.

"I know you don't want to, but I'm asking you to," he encourages.

I take a deep breath. "Honestly, I don't know why someone would want to distract us by setting it up like that. I think it could be to keep us away from Kaity so they can hurt her, but not even that makes a great deal of sense now that I'm thinking about it. So I guess I'm left with the one thought that I really don't want, and that's that all the things we've encountered, seem to lead back to me and my ordeal."

"So we can assume what, then?"

My heart pounds, my palms get sweaty, and my body trembles, but I answer him with what I think we both know is the truth.

"That whoever has her, possibly has her because of what I endured and they're trying to get back at me."

He nods, and his eyes are soft, comforting, understanding. "Exactly. So it makes sense then that Chris could possibly be telling the truth?"

I nod. Hating to agree, but agreeing all the same.

"So where do we go from here?"

"We dig deeper," I say softly, tired. "We look at it from a different angle."

"And what angle is that?"

"From me."

Me. It all comes back to me. But if I'm what will save my sister, if my story is what leads us to her, then I'll do whatever it takes.

He nods. "Yeah. You. I know I turned that thought from your head earlier, because I honestly didn't believe it could lead back to you, but I'm open to looking into it now, because I think you might be right."

"Yeah," I nod, tired.

"Do you feel any better?"

I do, because it helps me to process what happened with Chris and my emotions towards it. It helps me calm down and think clearer.

"I should shower," I say softly, standing. "Thank you."

My emotions are high. I just need to breathe.

"Always," he murmurs.

I smile and disappear into the shower. I need a few more moments to think. It's been a long, weary day. As the warm water washes over me, I think about Kaitlyn and wonder where she is. I think about the details Kenai and I just discussed. How all of Chris's associates painted him as a total dirtbag, but too stupid to be a serious criminal. They all told the same story as Chris: that he and Kaity had broken up a few days before she went missing, and then he quickly got out of town too. Which means we are on the right path now.

And someone else has her. Like I thought.

A tear rolls down my cheek, followed by another, and then another. My knees give way and I collapse onto the shower floor, sobbing uncontrollably. I can't stop it once it begins, and my sobs become wails as fear, panic, devastation, and loss cripple my body. Everything I've held in for so long, just comes out. Fear, guilt, weakness. It all just pours out. Like my body is just so damned tired of trying to keep it in.

I'm afraid. I'm lonely. I'm angry. I'm hurt. I'm paranoid. I'm so damned broken.

I don't hear the door open, I don't hear him step in, I just know a moment later strong arms wrap around me and pull me closer. My cheek slams against Kenai's chest and he holds on to me as I let it all go. Days of pent-up fear, years of pent-up emotional turmoil. He wraps his arms tighter, squeezing me until I feel like I can't breathe.

Exactly what I need and want.

"We're going to find her," he says, soaked from the warm water. "I swear it, Marlie. We'll find her."

"What if she's . . . what if she's already . . ."

"No," he says firmly. "No. Look at me."

He takes my chin in his hand and tilts my head back until I'm looking up at him. "Do not give up on her, do not give up on yourself, and do not give up on me."

My eyes lock with his and heat explodes inside my chest. I can't hold it back, I'm not even sure I want to. I reach up and swipe a piece of wet hair that's fallen over his eyes. I push it back and then tangle my fingers into the thick locks. I'm naked. In his arms. And I don't care. I bring my lips to his and press them in, hard.

"Marlie," he groans, running his fingers up my back. "Not a good idea."

I kiss him harder.

"Marlie," he growls, pushing me back a little. "Fuck. I can't. We can't."

Shame hits me right in the chest. I reel backwards, horror flashing across my features. Then I practically throw myself out of the shower. I'm horrified. He just rejected me. I put myself all in, and he rejected me.

"Marlie!" he calls after me as I wrap a towel around myself and rush out into the living room.

I start digging through my bag, looking for clothes, when he comes out with a towel wrapped around his waist. He has obviously discarded his wet clothes. Seeing him standing there, bare chest, dripping with water doesn't help.

"Marlie," he says carefully, moving closer.

"Don't," I growl, jerking out a pair of panties.

"I wasn't rejecting you."

I leap up, spinning around. "Weren't you?" I say, trying to keep it together, even though my chest feels like it's going to explode. "It's okay, Kenai. I get it. No worries."

"Christ," he grits out. "That is not why I pushed you away."

"Yeah," I mumble, pulling out a top. "It's okay, seriously."

"Just listen to me."

I ignore him, pulling out a pair of cotton shorts.

"Dammit, Marlie."

I straighten and start walking towards what I'm assuming is the bedroom.

"Stop," he orders.

"No," I snap.

I make it to the door just as his arm curls around mine and he jerks me back into his chest. His entire body is pressed against my back, and I can feel his hot breath against my neck as he growls, "Listen. To. Me."

"Eat a big fucking di—"

He spins me around so fast I nearly lose my footing, but he's holding me close and cradling my head in his hand so I'm fully supported. "I am not rejecting you."

"Pretty sure you are."

He reaches down between us and takes my hand, jerking it towards him and rubbing it against his cock. "Does that feel like I don't want to fuck you?"

I open my mouth, then close it again.

"Does it?" he hisses against my mouth. "Well?"

"No," I breathe.

"I want to fuck you so damned bad I can't think when I'm around you half the time. All I can do is imagine how good it would feel to have my cock sliding in and out of you. Hearing you scream my name. Feeling your pussy tightening around me."

I squeeze my legs together and a little gasp escapes my lips.

"So stop," he growls, coming closer, "running away from me."

"You said no," I say, staring at his lips.

"What I said was 'we can't.' It's not the same thing."

"Why can't we?"

His eyes flash. "Because you're paying me to do a job, and so far, I'm not doing it well enough. If I become distracted by you, I won't be able to do it to my full potential."

"It's one night, Kenai," I say, reaching forward and curling my hand around his cock.

"Marlie . . ."

"Please. I haven't been with anyone since . . . I . . . please?"

"Baby," he growls.

Baby.

My skin tingles.

I squeeze him.

"Fuck it," he hisses, reaching down and lifting my legs, hauling me up. I curl them around his hips and he slams my back against the wall. I moan and wrap my arms around his neck, pulling him in and capturing his lips with mine. He kisses me deep, hard, fast. Our tongues tangle, our lips smash together. We're desperate. It's radiating off both of us.

"Fuck," he rasps. "I can't wait, I don't even want to."

He reaches down between us and swipes his fingers through my pussy.

"So. Wet," he growls.

"Kenai," I whimper. "Please."

He thrusts a finger inside me, then another. A scream rips from my throat as I throw my head back, loving the way I stretch around him.

"Yes," he growls. "God, yes."

"Fuck me," I cry out, clutching his shoulders. "I need you to fuck me."

He thrusts a few more times with his fingers, then he slides them out and takes his cock, pressing it to my entrance. Then he slams upwards, filling me. I stretch around him, a pleasurable burn radiating through my body. It feels incredible. My fingernails find his back and I drag them down as he pulls out and slams back in.

My back hits the wall with a thump, and my moans intensify.

"You feel so good," I gasp as he fucks me with a ferocity I couldn't have even imagined in my wildest dreams.

"So tight," he moans, his fingers digging into my hips. "You're perfect, Marlie."

I whimper and tilt my hips, taking him deeper, needing him closer. "Kenai," I gasp.

"Fuck. Say that again."

"Kenai . . ."

He drives his cock deeper, harder, until my pussy is tightening around him and I can feel a raging orgasm building from the inside out. It starts right in my core, a warmth that quickly expands outwards until I feel like I can't possibly take it anymore.

I come hard.

So hard I can't hear my own screams.

Kenai bellows and then his body comes to a stop and I can feel every pulse as he finds his release, too.

I drop my head into his shoulder and exhale loudly, then I take a few moments to just breathe him in. He smells incredible. Whatever cologne he's wearing drives me wild. That smell, mixed with his own unique scent, is enough to send any woman over the edge.

"That was incredible," he murmurs, releasing me. I keep my face close to him, though. I need just a few more moments.

"God, it really was," I whisper against his skin.

"Let me take a shower, again, and then we'll get something to eat."

I nod and step back on shaky legs.

His eyes find me and something passes between us.

Something incredible.

Something intense.

Something real.

"Tell me something about yourself," I ask Kenai later as we lie side by side in the bed, our feet touching, my hand resting in his. "Something nobody knows."

"I had a sister," he says, stroking his thumb over my palm.

My heart beats harder. "Had?"

"She died."

My stomach twists and my heart skips a beat. I couldn't imagine. I couldn't . . . not even for a second . . . imagine how that must have felt. The fear of losing my sister is enough to send me over the edge emotionally, but to actually lose her. My heart aches for him.

"I'm so sorry. Can I ask what happened?"

His thumb stops stroking, and he goes still for a moment. I'm worried I've asked too much, but a second later he starts talking. "She went missing. She was only fourteen. She was there one minute, gone the next. She was with me. She said she was going to the store. She never came home."

My skin prickles and I roll to my side, looking at him. "I'm so sorry, Kenai."

"I should have been watching her, but I was too busy hanging with some stupid girl. She went alone, some creep got hold of her and killed her."

A flood of horror washes through my body. I know how that feels. I know what it's like to be in the hands of a monster.

"It's not your fault," I say softly. "There are horrible people out there. It wouldn't have mattered what you did."

"I was her older brother; I should have been there with her."

"She went to the store, Kenai. You didn't leave

her in a deserted forest. There were people around. You couldn't have kept your eye on her every second. It isn't your fault."

He says nothing, and his body is so stiff. I'm not going to push. I know how it feels to have people push when you just want to be left alone.

"Did you find the man that did it?"

He nods. "Yeah, they found him. He killed himself in prison."

Thank God.

"Is that why you do what you do?"

He rolls so he's facing me. I can see the pain behind his eyes, and I want to reach out and take it away. "Yeah. I watched the police try to find her, I watched them and all I could think was 'they're not doing enough.' I knew in that moment what I was going to do. I was going to go above and beyond to find people."

"And you made it your entire life."

"Yeah," he says, reaching over and swiping a piece of hair from my forehead.

"I'm sorry that happened to your sister."

He smiles, it's weak but it's there.

"It's why you were so angry at me when you thought I had something to do with that book, isn't it?"

His eyes flash and his jaw tightens, but he nods. "I didn't know at the time you had no involvement. I thought you used your ordeal to get your claim to fame and it made me so angry. I couldn't understand how anyone could do something like that, when so many others were out there, missing or being tortured. I also didn't fully understand what you'd been through. It was easier for me to judge you instead of thinking about what you suffered. And I'm sorry for that, Marlie. "

"It's okay," I say, my voice shaky. "I've hated every second of that book. It's ruined my life. It's ruined Kaity's life. I wish my mother had done more to help me and Kaity instead of throwing us into the spotlight."

"You can't change selfish people, Marlie. You can only choose to be better."

"I just hate that Kaity suffered for it. If it wasn't for my ordeal and that damned book."

"Don't," he says, his voice hardening just slightly. "Don't blame yourself. You didn't ask for any of it. Kaity suffered, I understand that, but she still made her own choices. You can't always blame yourself for other people's mistakes and decisions. In the end, we're adults and we still make the final decision on how we pave our life path."

I shuffle closer and press my lips to his. "You should take your own advice."

He snorts.

"Admit it," I say, curling my arms around his neck. "You like me now."

He grumbles and pulls me closer. "Just a tiny bit."

My smile just about splits my face.

And it feels incredible.

FIFTEEN

I fall asleep in Kenai's arms after talking for hours, but I'm woken sometime during the night to a rustling sound outside. I reach for my cell phone to see what time it is, but when I don't find it, I remember I left it in the car. As much as I want to stay snuggled in bed, I want to check to see if anyone has called or texted about Kaity. I roll out of Kenai's arms carefully and I pull on a tank top and a soft pair of cotton shorts.

I glance back down at Kenai, but he's sound asleep and I know he's exhausted. I don't want to wake him.

I walk towards the door that leads out the back of the cabin. I flick the outside light on and step out, peering around. I can't see anything, so I take another shaky step. The rustling comes from my left, and I whip my head in that direction, saying softly, "Hello?"

Nothing.

Probably just a squirrel.

I'm about to turn around and head back inside when I see that the interior light of Kenai's truck is on. Narrowing my eyes, I move towards it hesitantly. Something feels off, but I remember Kenai's words about me being paranoid. He probably just left the door open when he brought our bags in. I head over to close it. I reach the truck and see the passenger door is ajar. My blood runs cold.

That doesn't seem right. One door, maybe. Two . . . no. My body goes on high alert as I peer around.

It's only then I realize it's dark out here. Really, really dark.

I turn and face the cabin when a noise sounds out to my right. It's loud, really loud, and it sounds an awful lot like footsteps. "Kenai?" I whisper, pressing my back to the truck.

The footsteps near, but I can't see anyone. My heart is thudding against my rib cage as I start moving towards the back of the truck. "Kenai, is that you?"

A branch snaps, loud and terrifying.

I don't think, I just turn and run.

I start towards the cabin, but a shadow right next to it has me swiveling in the opposite direction. As I charge into the trees I can hear the footsteps behind me quicken. Someone is chasing me. An all too familiar fear creeps up my spine. I run faster, tree branches scratching my arms, logs tripping me.

My hands hit the dirt when I go down over a fallen tree. I scurry forwards and my forehead slams into a thick tree trunk. Fear clogs my throat and I start sobbing, crawling forwards, fingers burning as skin is torn from them. The footsteps get closer, and I know I have to get up. I have to.

Get up.

Run, Marlie.

I push to my feet and start running again, hitting trees, dodging rocks. Blood trickles down my face and I can taste the coppery scent in my mouth. "Leave me alone!" I scream, panting, knees throbbing.

The footsteps get quicker and my knees give way.

I fall forward, pain radiating through them, right up my spine. I scream and try to scurry forward, but a heavy body lands flat on my back, pushing my face down into the dirt. I can't tell if it's male or female, I can't tell anything. A hand hits the back of my head and shoves my face into the dirt.

I fight.

I squirm and buck.

"Let me go!" I scream.

"Marlie?"

Kenai.

Oh God.

"Where are you?" I hear his frantic voice getting closer.

A chilling voice masked by a voice changer radiates through my ear. "It's not over. It's just beginning. I hope you missed me, Marlie. I'm watching."

Then the body lifts off me and footsteps disappear into the trees.

I can't move.

I can't breathe.

Was it him? Is he alive? Oh God. He's alive. He's alive.

I don't realize I'm screaming until Kenai falls to his knees in front of me, grabbing me and pulling me into his arms. "What happened? Marlie, what happened?"

"H-H-H-H-H-H-He . . ."

"Calm down and talk to me. Fuck, you're bleeding."

"He's . . . he's . . ."

"Marlie, breathe."

"He's alive," I whisper,

Kenai's body goes still.

Then he scoops me into his arms and says quietly, "Let's get you inside."

He flashes his light around, but there is no one in sight.

He's gone.

For now.

* * *

"Marlie, talk to me," Kenai says, squatting in front of me, washing my dirty face with a warm cloth.

"It was him."

"Who?"

My eyes meet his and they flare.

"Marlie, he's dead."

"It was him, Kenai. I know it. I've known it all along. He's got Kaity and he's tormenting me. This is all a game. A trick. He lured me out to that truck and he chased me through the woods. If you didn't come out . . ."

"Did you see him?" Kenai asks, carefully, gently. I blink. "No, but . . ."

"Did you hear his voice when he spoke to you?"

"He had one of those voice-changer things on. I know what I heard, Kenai. He said it's not over."

Kenai studies me, and I can see the pity in his eyes. He's looking at me like he feels sorry for me.

"Did you have a dream before you went outside?"

My eyes widen. "You think I imagined it?"

He takes my hand but I jerk it back. "I didn't imagine it," I cry, horrified he'd even think that.

"Marlie, sometimes when stress and emotions are high, our bodies do strange things. Have flashbacks. It's a form of PTSD."

"It was real, I didn't chase myself through the woods," I yell, standing up, legs shaking.

"Please don't get upset," he says, carefully, controlled, like he's talking to a woman who is about to dive off a cliff.

"I know what I saw, I know what I felt, I know what I heard. Someone was out there tonight, Kenai. Someone tormented me. Someone is playing a game. Until you believe me, until you're willing to look at this from my side, we're never going to be safe. And neither is Kaity. Think what you want about me, and maybe I do have PTSD. But that did not cause this. This really happened. I can tell the difference."

I turn and rush into the bedroom, my entire body aching, my heart full of fear at my nightmare being reopened. I can't believe Kenai thinks I'm imagining things, that he refuses to consider that The Watcher is involved. Why can't he see that I'm telling the truth? Why can't he believe in me enough to know that I know with every single ounce of my being that this is connected to my past?

"Hey."

I turn from my spot on the bed twenty minutes later and see Kenai walking in, a tablet in his hands.

"Please don't, I can't take anymore."

"I went outside, looked on the ground. You were right. There are two sets of footprints. I'm sorry. I should have believed you."

I nod, but my throat tightens.

"I've got all my notes and police documents here, from your case, from Kaity's, everything. I think we need to start again. I think we've been looking at this all wrong."

"I think so too," I say, shifting over on the bed so he can sit beside me.

"You up for a long night? This could take a while."

I shrug and peer over his shoulder at the screen. "I wouldn't be able to sleep anyway. I'll make us some coffee."

"Before we do this, let me finish cleaning you up. You've still got blood and dirt on your face."

I nod weakly.

He stands and extends a hand to me. I narrow my eyes and shake my head in confusion.

"Trust me?"

I reach out and take his hand. He pulls me to my feet and leads me to the bathroom. He lets me go and turns the shower on, then he turns back towards me and murmurs in a low, husky voice, "Arms up."

I lift my arms and he takes the hem of my shirt, slowly lifting it up and over my head. My heart pounds against my ribcage as he tosses the shirt to the side and his hands come back to rest against my skin. I look up at him, my eyes holding his as he reaches down and slides my shorts down. I tremble as I stand before him naked, holding his eyes, loving the way he stares at me.

"You're beautiful, Marlie."

My cheeks heat as he removes his clothes and then carefully takes my hand and pulls me into the shower. The first touch of the water against my skin has a hiss leaving my lips. It burns the tiny scratches and cuts all over my body. Kenai takes a soft washer and soaks it with water, before stepping forward and gently wiping the dirt and blood from my face.

I say nothing.

Neither of us do.

You don't need to say a single word to understand what another person feels. Sometimes you can sense it with every fiber of your being, just by looking at them. It's an energy that passes between you. A deep understanding. A bond. It's real. It's pure. You know it with every single piece of who you are. No, words are not needed when you have a connection that reaches your soul.

I reach out and stroke my fingers against his skin, running them down his chest and over his abs. He shudders beneath my touch, but does nothing to stop me. I think we're both well and truly past trying to fight this. I drop lower, curling my hand around his cock. He makes a low, feral sound in his throat and growls, "Baby, believe me, I want this again but you're hurt and I'm not that big of a dog."

I raise up on my tiptoes and whisper, "I didn't say I was going to get anything, maybe I just want something for you."

His eyes flash as I lower down to my knees, keeping my fingers curled around his cock. The warm water trails over me and my knees burn, but

I don't stop, I don't even want to. I bring him to my lips and take him in, swirling my tongue around the tip, loving how he hisses and bucks his hips.

"Dammit, yes," he rasps, putting his hands up onto the shower wall as I take him deeper.

I curl my hand around the base, stroking as I suck, loving the sounds that leave his lips, loving how it feels to have him under my control. He tangles his fingers gently in my hair and guides my mouth deeper down onto his cock. It feels good, incredible, even though my scalp burns a little from the pressure. But this is one moment when I'm not going to let the demons of my past haunt me.

"I'm going to come," he growls. "God, Marlie. Fuck yes."

He moans low and throaty as he releases into my mouth. I take all of him, loving how he tastes, how he feels. I gently pull back and look up, finding his dark, lusty eyes. He reaches down and cups my jaw, murmuring, "You're perfect."

A loud crash has both our heads whipping around.

Kenai moves fast. "Don't move."

He's out of the shower with a towel wrapped around him before I can even push off my knees. Another crash. Then a loud, angry curse.

I get up and rush out of the shower, pulling a towel around me and running out into the living room. I can't believe we let ourselves get distracted.

Guilt swarms my chest as I move through the living room. Kenai is nowhere to be seen, and the kitchen table is turned over, all the contents from the top scattered across the floor.

All of the contents except . . . Kenai's tablet.

"Kenai?" I call frantically, rushing to the front door.

He's out in the woods, head whipping back and forth as he barks, "I'll find you. I don't need my files to do that."

Then he turns and charges back up to the house, fists clenched, mouth tight with anger.

"Kenai?" I say softly, clutching the towel tighter against myself.

"Someone doesn't want us investigating any further. You're right, we're being played with. It's not safe here. We need to go."

I nod, turning and rushing back into the house. Kenai gets dressed as quickly as I do, and we gather our things before rushing out to the truck. When we reach it, Kenai puts an arm up, halting me. His eyes narrow and he murmurs, "Stay here."

He moves towards the truck and I notice the back door is ajar. He doesn't swing it open, but instead gets on his hands and knees and looks under the truck. I watch him with confusion as he scours the entire truck. Standing, he moves to the other door and pulls it open, then his entire body goes stiff.

"Kenai?" I call, taking a step forward.

He reaches and lifts something, then he turns

and looks at me. There is sympathy in his eyes. Pity, even.

"What is it?"

He steps out. In his hand he has a lock of thick red hair tied with a ribbon. *No. Please. No.*

"That's his trademark," I gasp. I can't breathe. I can't seem to get my lungs to even try and work. "And that's Kaity's hair!"

My world starts spinning and Kenai moves quickly, catching me around the waist before I can fall. I bury my face into his shirt and take a few deep, calming breaths. I can't lose it. I can't. That's what whoever this is wants. They're trying to scare me. Trying to get me to break. They won't win. I won't let them.

I pull back and meet Kenai's eyes. "We need to find her, Kenai. I know what he's doing to her. We have to help her."

"It's not him, Marlie."

I open my mouth to argue, but he puts up a hand.

"I'm not saying you're crazy," he continues. "I'm just saying it's not him. He's dead. I saw all the reports. Whoever this is, he's a copycat."

"A . . . copycat?" I say, rubbing my arms to try to remove the chill from my body.

"Yes, a copycat. A disturbed stranger who read your book and got a sick idea. Either way, it's not him."

"How can you be so sure?"

He leans down, lifting the bag off the floor.

"Copycats are a lot more common than the dead coming back to life. And The Watcher is dead—I've read the autopsy reports, seen pictures of his body."

"Were your files backed up? How are we supposed to find out anything without them?"

"We're heading back to Vegas today. I have a friend in the police force there, he'll help me regain access to the information."

"And Kaity?" I say in a scared voice, my eyes falling to the lock of thick red hair resting in his hands.

"We're going to find her. Do you trust me?"

I look up at him, and nod. "Always."

"Then let's go. We're running out of time."

SIXTEEN

We reach Vegas a little after lunch. Kenai parks in front of a local police station, and we both head inside. There is a pretty young blonde at the reception desk, happily chatting away on the phone. When she looks up and sees Kenai, her face splits into a massive grin. She says a quick goodbye, then leaps up and charges at him. "Kenai!" she squeals, launching into his arms.

My brows shoot up.

"Hi, Sara, long time no see. How are you sweetheart?"

Sweetheart?

My chest clenches. Is that jealousy?

I squash it down.

"I'm good now," she says. "You look great."

"So do you. How are Mark and the kids?"

She's married.

Down, tiger.

I relax.

"They're all good. The boys are both in school now."

"No kidding?" Kenai grins. "Nice. Hey, is Darcy in?"

"He is. He'll be thrilled you're here. I'll call him out."

She goes back around the desk as Kenai turns to look at me. Then he grins.

"What?" I ask, crossing my arms.

"You were jealous."

I snort. "As if."

"You were. I saw it."

"Don't flatter yourself, Fabio. I was curious. Not jealous."

His grin gets bigger.

I roll my eyes and turn back towards the counter. A moment later a gorgeous man comes out with Sara. He's tall, dark, and handsome. He's not rugged, like Kenai, but more sophisticated and clean cut. His hair is slicked back, his eyes are almond-shaped and brown, and he's got a grin on his face, showcasing two stunning dimples.

"Kenai, brother," he laughs, walking over and throwing his arms around Kenai. "Long time no see."

"Still looking sharp, Darcy," Kenai chuckles, stepping back. "How's things?"

"Better now that you're here"—Darcy's eyes flick to me and widen—"Marlie Jacobson."

Great.

He knows me.

"Hi," I say softly.

Darcy walks over and extends a hand. "It's an absolute honor to meet you. I've heard your story, as I'm sure most have. I'm awed by your strength and courage."

The compassion in his eyes puts me at ease. "Move over, Kenai," I say, taking Darcy's hand, "I just fell in love."

Darcy bursts out laughing as Kenai mumbles something under his breath.

"I like her. If you don't keep her for yourself, let me know." Darcy winks, then lets my hand go. "What can I do for you?"

"First," Kenai grumbles, "you can stop hitting on her. She isn't available. But you can give me some information."

Is Kenai . . . jealous? My heart flutters.

My legs tremble but I keep it together. I know they can both see the blush that crawls up my cheeks, though.

Darcy's grin gets bigger and he wiggles his brows before turning and saying, "Follow me."

We move down the hall after him, the intensity between us now at an all-time high. We just about slam into each other trying to get into Darcy's office.

"You two are hilarious," Darcy chuckles, sitting down behind his desk.

Kenai shoots him a glare.

I giggle.

Kenai shoots me a glare.

Moody.

"So, what can I do for you?" Darcy asks when we both sit down.

"Need the files on Marlie's case and The Watcher. Mine were stored securely but my device was lost, and I can't access them remotely. Need to go over them."

Darcy taps his fingers on his chin. "Not my department, you know that. The crime happened in Denver."

"Yeah, but I know you have contacts and can get me the information."

"I can, but not until you tell me why."

I look to Kenai, but he holds Darcy's stare.

"Remember that time I pulled you out of the shit . . ."

Darcy rolls his eyes. "All right. I knew you'd use that against me." He hands Kenai a slip of paper. "Write down the case information, then give me until this afternoon. I'll get you copies of the files."

Kenai scrawls down what he can and hands the paper back to Darcy. "Good man," Kenai says, standing. "If you're not busy later, have a drink with us."

Darcy looks to me then to Kenai, and chuckles, "It's not me who will be busy."

I roll my eyes. I can't hold back my smile.

I feel immediately guilty for letting myself feel

good, but at the same time, a little bit of light in this dark situation is exactly what we need.

Sometimes you just need a little bit of good.

"You don't want to look at these, sweetheart," Kenai murmurs, flicking through the paper copy of the files that Darcy dropped off an hour ago. "Since we're dealing with a copycat, I had Darcy pull files from the original case too."

"It's nothing I haven't seen," I say, trying to peek around him.

"Maybe, but you don't need to relive this horror. Let me go through them."

"Kenai, please, I need to help. Don't give me the picture files, just the information files. I'll look over those."

He looks up, studies me, then mutters, "You won't leave me alone until I give them to you, will you?"

I shake my head with a grin.

He grunts and hands me a stack of papers. "All the information on Clayton. See what you can find out. Family. Friends. Anything."

Clayton. The Watcher.

My skin prickles, but I take a deep breath and open the file, reading his information. Name. Birthdate. Weight. Skin Color. Hair Color. Eye Color. Previous criminal records, which honestly didn't hold much except a few charges for breaking and entering that couldn't be proven. My throat is tight as I scour the information. I didn't know all of this. I wonder if the police ever looked back on his file and thought about the times he came in for minor crimes and wondered if they might have looked at him a little harder? Would they have known? Do any of us really know if we're having an encounter with a killer?

I flick through the first few pages, and then come across a couple of notes in scrawly hand-writing. They look like someone just thinking out loud.

Clayton grew up in San Diego? Family?

I keep reading the scribbled notes that officers have obviously added throughout the investigations.

Information on his parents is scarce. Suspect was put into the foster system right from birth.

I swallow. The foster system from birth. Is that why he turned out the way he did?

Interview with foster families reveal that he had a long history of violence. At one point was caught cross-dressing.

I shiver. I remember the way he was so obsessed with females and their beauty.

No word on parents still, but have located information that says he has a sister who was put into the system a few years before him.

A sister.

He has a sister.

"Here!" I cry, looking up.

Kenai jerks and looks up from his scouring. "What?"

"He has a sister. She might know something."

I hand the paper to Kenai, and he nods, giving me a proud expression. "Good lead. See if you can find out if they discovered who she is, or even where she lives."

I keep reading intently.

Sister is said to live in San Diego still. Alone. Not married. She claimed she hadn't seen her brother since he was a child. No evidence suggests she is aware of his crimes. Questioned her. She was unable to provide any useful information.

"She lives in San Diego, they questioned her but she claimed she hadn't seen Clayton since he was a child," I say, still reading.

"That's likely, especially in the foster system. You get a name?"

I keep reading, running my finger down the page until I spot it.

"Georgia Dumas. There's an address."

Kenai grins at me. "Nice work, baby. You might have a future in detective work."

I smile and huff. "I doubt it, considering all I did was read a file."

"You did good."

"So, are we going to pay Georgia a visit?"

Kenai nods, closing the file. "We most certainly are, but for right now, I'm taking you to bed."

My cheeks heat.

I drop the file.

Sounds perfect to me.

SEVENTEEN

"Fuck," Kenai growls, running a hand through his hair.

We both stare at his truck. The tires are slashed, the windows broken, but it's the words I'M WATCHING spray-painted along the side that get to us the most. Whoever has my sister, they're smart and they're close. And whoever it is, is obviously following us.

"What do we do now?" I ask, rubbing the chills from my arms.

"We'll hire a car."

"He's watching us," I say, tucking myself into Kenai's side as my eyes scan the parking lot.

"Yeah, we're being watched. We need to be more careful. Whoever it is doesn't want us figuring this out. They like the game. Most killers do."

"Do you think he was listening last night?"

"Possibly. I guess we'll find out when we arrive at Georgia's house. Right now, we need to keep our eyes open. We're not safe."

I nod and stick to Kenai's side as we move out onto the street and flag down a cab. It takes us to a car rental company where we get ready to hit the road. The entire drive back towards California passes in silence. My mind is spinning with the possibilities. Whoever is following us is clever. I continually look behind us, staring into all the cars following, wondering which one he or she is in.

My phone rings, jerking me out of my thoughts. It's Hannah. I haven't called her for a few days.

"Hey," I say, answering in a tired voice.

"Hey. I was just checking in on you. I haven't heard from you in a few days. You okay? Is everything going well?"

I sigh. "Not really. Turns out Chris isn't the one who has Kaity."

She gasps. "What do you mean?"

"We got to LA and found out we'd been led down the wrong path."

"Who would do that?"

My eyes flick to Kenai, and he shakes his head. He doesn't want me to say anything.

"We're not sure yet, but we're going back over the case now."

"Poor Kaity," Hannah says, her voice worried. "I can only imagine what she's going through right now."

Guilt and fear go to war in my chest and I mumble, "Yeah."

"I just wanted to check in on you, see how you were. I know this must be hard for you."

"It is," I admit. "I'm terrified for her."

"I would be, too."

"Anyway, I have to go, Han. I'll keep you updated."

"Stay safe, Marlie. I don't want you to get hurt again, too."

"I won't. Bye."

I hang up and turn to Kenai.

"Sorry," he says. "Don't want anyone knowing what we're doing, not when we're being watched. You could be putting anyone you tell in danger."

Of course.

I can't believe I didn't think of that. "Of course. Thank you."

"Hannah hasn't heard anything?"

I shake my head. "No. She's just worried, like the rest of us."

"Has your mom called again?"

I grunt. "Yeah right. She's too busy trying to make more money."

Kenai shakes his head, and points left into a gas station. "We'll fill up, get some food, and get as far as we can tonight."

I nod as he parks. "I have to pee anyway."

I climb out of the car and move towards the building while Kenai starts filling up. There aren't many people around. I stare into the window as I pass and see an elderly man at the counter. He stares at me, and I give him a small smile. I have a funny feeling in my stomach, but I move towards the restrooms, which are in a large brick building at the back of the station.

I duck into the ladies room, and scrunch my nose. It obviously hasn't been cleaned for a long time. I'm starting to wonder if I would have been better off squatting under a tree. I pick the cleanest of the three toilets and line the seat with toilet paper. Then I quickly do my business. Just then, I hear the outside door slam shut and see the lights flick out. The entire restroom goes dark. There are no windows. It's old and made of cinderblocks. My heart leaps into my throat and I stand. "Hello?"

I can't hear anything for a few seconds.

Then I hear it.

"Brush it, Marlie. That's Sasha's pretty hair. Pretend Sasha is here, pretend you're having a little girls party. What would you say to her?"

No.

Oh God.

The recording continues, filling the restroom. Hearing his voice is like a punch to the gut. My knees tremble. I reach for the door to let myself out, but I can't move it. I bang against it, fists pounding. "Let me out!" I scream.

"I-I-I'd say—"

"Don't talk to me, Marlie, talk to Sasha. Ask her about the boy she's seeing."

"Are you still seeing that boy, Sasha?"

"Very good. What would Sasha say back?"

"Let me out!" I bellow, hammering my fists against the door. "Let me go."

The horrible recording of my nightmare continues.

"I-I-I'd say, he's so good looking, don't you think?"

"Keep going. What else would you say to Sasha about the boy she likes?"

"I think he's very handsome. Do you?"

"Make her tell you what she's going to do with him."

Something moves outside the door, then something is tossed over the top of the stall, landing right on top of me. It's a lock of thick hair. I scream and scramble backwards, falling against the toilet. The hair is black, and it has the scalp attached, just like he used to keep them. My screams turn hysterical as I try to claw my way out of the stall. The door is jammed.

"Kenai!" I scream.

I scream and scream, even after the door slams open. I keep screaming until my voice is hoarse and my legs give way. I fall to the ground and a second later something shifts and Kenai appears in the doorway, eyes dropping to the ground.

"No," he rasps, reaching for me and lifting me into his arms.

"He was here again," I wail. "I could hear a r-r-r-recording of me and him . . . when he had me. Then . . . that . . ."

Kenai's eyes drop to the scalp and the horror that washes over his features matches my own. He carries me outside while looking around to see if he can see anyone, carefully placing me on my feet on the soft grass. He swipes my tear dampened hair from my face and cups my cheeks in his hands. "Breathe, real deep."

Panic seizes my chest. "He's going to find me. He's going to get me. He's going to—"

The all too familiar tightening in my chest lets me know a panic attack is about to hit full force. I press the back of my hand to my mouth to try to stifle my terrified moan of pain.

"Marlie, breathe, with me, come on."

He inhales and I try to shakily copy him.

Then he exhales.

We do this until my breathing gets back to normal and my tears dry up. The owner of the gas station came out to ask if there was a problem. Kenai told him I was car sick, and he shrugged and went back inside.

"I'm going to go back in there and check it out. Stand here, call out to me if you need me."

I nod, wrapping my arms around myself.

Kenai goes back into the restroom while I look around. It seems deserted, yet I know he's out there somewhere, watching, waiting.

"You won't beat me down," I say softly to myself. "Not this time."

Not this time.

"There was a note attached to it," Kenai says later that night after we've stopped for the evening.

I'm sitting on the bed in the hotel room, but my head whips up when he says that. "There was? What did it say?"

He reaches into his pocket and pulls out a small slip of paper. I don't know what he did with the hair, and I don't care. He said he took care of it, and that's all I need to know. I didn't know there was a note, however. I extend my hand, but he hesitates.

"I can handle it, Kenai. I know I freaked out back there, but I'm not going to let this beat me. I won't let him win. Please."

He sighs and stands, then walks over and places the note in my hand.

I unfold it and read the scrawly writing.

I'm watching you. Always.
Your hair will look lovely next to
your sister's.

I scrunch the note in my fist and fight down the goose bumps that rise all over my skin. "Oh God . . ."

"It's a threat. Don't let it get to you, Marlie."

"What if Kaity's already . . . already . . ."

"Hey," he says, coming over and sitting beside me. "Don't let him win. We're going to find her, and we're going to end this once and for all."

"It just doesn't make sense," I say, tucking my legs beneath me. "Why not just take me? Obviously whoever this is, is more interested in me."

"It's a game," Kenai says, walking over and dropping down onto the bed beside me. "It's a mindfuck. Whoever it is took your sister for revenge, I'd guess."

"Do you still think it's a copycat? Or do you think it's possible that Clayton wasn't really killed."

"I think letting us believe Kaity was taken by Chris was a way of upping the stakes, freaking us out, getting our minds working, and possibly buying time. Now the game has shifted; now it's become focused on tormenting you."

"Do you think Kaity is safe then?"

He shakes his head. "No. If anything, I worry she's in more danger because she's being used as bait."

I shudder. "Do you think this could be Georgia, Clayton's sister?"

Kenai shrugs. "I'm not sure. What I am sure of though, is that whoever it is has some connection to Clayton. Questioning Georgia is a good place to start. She might be able to tell us something about their parents or about any family members they were close to before they were put into the foster care system."

"Do you think it could be a close friend from the foster home?"

"Possibly. We'll explore that angle too, once we know more about his birth family."

"I'm scared, Kenai," I whisper.

He pulls me into his arms. "I know you are, but I need you to be strong. Can you do that? I'm not going to let anyone hurt you, sweetheart."

"I know."

"You trust me?"

I nestle closer. "Always."

EIGHTEEN

"Are you sure we're on the right path?" I ask, narrowing my eyes as Kenai turns down a dirt road a good distance out of town.

"Yep, I've confirmed the address. This is the right way."

"So his sister lives out of town?"

Kenai nods. "Seems so. San Diego is pretty big."

We keep driving down the long, deserted dirt road until we reach an old cottage set amongst some large trees. "Here it is," Kenai murmurs.

I get a tremble as I study the old, run-down place. It doesn't look lived in. It looks like it's barely standing. "It doesn't look like anyone lives here," I say.

"Looks can be deceiving," he responds, stopping the car and climbing out. "You coming?"

I stare at the house. It's old, so old there are

pieces of weatherboard hanging off the side. The paint is faded and cracked. The roof looks like half of it had been torn off at some point and was hastily slapped back on. It's the scariest, most awful house I've ever seen.

I take a deep breath then shove the door open and climb out. I'm not sure if I'm ready to come face-to-face with Clayton's sister, with someone who is related to him, someone who shares his blood. Was she close with her brother? Will she know who I am? Will she even want to help us?

I take Kenai's hand as we move closer, but he comes to a stop before we even reach the door. It takes me a moment to realize why.

"What is that smell?" I whisper, pressing my free hand to my nose.

"I'd know that anywhere. Stay here."

"Kenai—"

"Stay here, Marlie."

I do as he says, stopping as he goes up onto the little front porch and disappears into the house. He's in there a few minutes, and the entire time, I'm scanning the area around us, wondering if we're being watched. Nervously, I rub my arms until he finally comes back out with his hand pressed over his nose. "She's dead."

I blink. "What?"

"His sister's dead, if that's his sister in there. Gunshot to the head. Zero struggle. Whoever killed her knew her, and she wasn't suspecting it.

I've covered the body. I need to search the house. You want to wait out here?"

I shake my head. "No, I can handle it. I want to help you. I know Kaity's things—if there's any chance there is something of hers lying around here, I'll be able to tell you."

He nods.

I follow him into the house.

The smell is out of this world. I find a cloth in a kitchen cupboard and press it to my nose while I avoid looking at the body under the sheet. There is blood on the floor beside it. I avoid looking at that, too.

"I'll check the bedroom," I say, moving in that direction.

It's a tiny space, with an old rusted bed and a cheap desk in the corner. There are no curtains and the window looks like it's been left open for a long time. I don't know the woman, but this isn't a way for anyone to live. I carefully walk across the floor, which is partially covered in a shaggy, dirty rug. I go to the bed first and pull back the covers. Dirty sheets. Nothing else.

I look beneath it. Dust. Nothing else.

I move to the desk and open drawers and cupboards and flick through papers. There isn't anything of interest here except a couple of bills and some old books. I open them, flicking through the pages to make sure nothing is hidden there. All of a sudden a tiny key drops out. I reach down and pick up the rusted little object. I glance around the room, trying to figure out what it unlocks. Nothing on the desk is lockable.

I do three slow laps around the room, then go back to the desk. It has to be the desk. I take it and use all my strength to pull it towards me. I then duck around behind it and see a tiny compartment in the back with a keyhole. I squeeze into the tight space, slide the key in, and unlock the door. Inside is an old, well-worn diary. I squeeze back out and go sit on the bed. I open the diary to a random page and begin to read.

Dear Diary,

He's gone again. I know what he's doing. I always know what he's doing. I'm so afraid. For him. For our child. For me. I know I should do something, but I'm so scared of how he'll react. He's already corrupted her. Today she came to me with a dead mouse—she had peeled its skin from its body. I'm terrified the devil is already in her. How can he not be? She was born into this world evil, and nothing I can do seems to be able to protect her.

I'm so afraid.

I'm so trapped.

My throat tightens. I open up another random section.

Dear Diary,

She scares me. My own daughter scares me. It's his fault. Or maybe it's mine. A child born through incest, of course she was going to be evil. I had no choice. He forced himself on me. I could do nothing to stop it. Now another monster is being created. I think she's worse. I can see it in her eyes. I can see the evil he has created. He's so proud of her. So proud of the disturbing thoughts coming from her mind.

Today she threw a knife at me.

They both laughed.

I'm so afraid.

Oh. My. God.

I rub my chest, trying to stop the vomit from rising. Clayton raped his own sister, and they had a child together. A child. An evil child.

That poor, poor woman.

I flick to the last page, wondering about the date of the last entry. It was three days ago.

Dear Diary,

She's gone, but she'll be back.

I know this is the end. She's evil by blood and by nature. She wants to follow in his footsteps. She wants revenge. She can't see any wrong. When he died, all she could do was hate. She said nobody understood. She said her father wasn't the monster, that those girls were the monsters. She believes it. She believes in his evil. I can't live like this anymore. I can't live with her threats. I can't live knowing what kind of monster my child has turned into.

I know she'll be back.

Any day now.

And I know that this time, she'll kill me.

I welcome it. I'm ready to escape this nightmare.

Tears run down my face, and I swipe them away. Her own daughter killed her.

"What is it?"

I look up to see Kenai coming in, papers and books in his hands.

"He has a daughter, a daughter he had with his own sister. I found a diary, her diary." I point towards the living room. "She expresses how afraid she was, how evil her daughter is, how she's just like her father. In the last entry she said she knows that she's going to kill her, and she welcomes it. Her own daughter killed her. Clayton has a replica of him out there somewhere."

Kenai looks horrified. "It's his daughter doing this?"

"I think so," I whisper. "We need to find her."

Kenai nods. "I got as much as I can, let's get out of here."

"What about the body?"

Kenai shakes his head. "Let me worry about that. Let's just leave. I have a bad feeling about this place."

I nod and stand, pressing the diary to my chest and rushing out after Kenai. As I pass the body, I feel pity and a small sense of relief for the woman lying there.

At least she's free now.

It seems our nightmare, however, is only just starting.

NINETEEN

I read the diary the entire way back to the hotel. I can't take my eyes off the horror that's unfolding before me. This poor woman, what she lived through, it makes my skin crawl. I can't imagine living that way, with those kinds of demons. Kenai sits quietly, letting me devour the journal like it's a novel, only occasionally asking me to let him know if anything stands out. One particular entry has my skin crawling.

Dear Diary,

They're obsessed with my hair. Every day he makes me sit while he runs his fingers through it. He's teaching her. Showing her. He tells her how hair should look, how it should feel, how long it should be, and how soft it should be. He criticizes me if mine doesn't look pretty enough, or if it isn't washed. He's obsessed with hair.

Today, he made me sit for three hours while he demonstrated exactly how the hair is attached to the scalp, and how easily it is removed with the right technique. Hearing her laugh as he explained it, listening to them talk about it as if it were nothing more than a discussion about a car, frightened me.

But I sat. And I let them.

I'm going to regret this one day. I'm helping to create two monsters that nobody will escape from.

Why am I so weak? Why don't I just run?

God help me.

I shiver and try to focus on the facts that are important. "The strange thing," I say, closing the diary, "is that she never mentions the daughter's name, not even once. It's like she was too afraid to even put it in here, like somehow it could come back and haunt her."

"It's not uncommon for people to skip over names in diary entries, just for safety and privacy reasons. Georgia had told the police she knew nothing about her brother, which was clearly a lie. I guess she couldn't face the truth so she kept it hidden, so no one would find out."

I nod, exhaling loudly. "I just can't believe her own brother did that to her, and then forced her to raise a child created from incest."

"Yeah, it's fucking sad," Kenai says, his voice low. "Just makes you realize there are sick people out there, sicker than you can ever imagine."

"Do you think you'll be able to find anything when we get back to the hotel?"

He shrugs. "I'm not sure, I collected what I could and I'll look into her medical records to see if there is any reference to this child, but honestly, I'm guessing the child was never even registered."

"Can you imagine the life she lived? The child, I mean?"

Kenai nods. "Yeah, it couldn't have been pleasant."

"Do you think people can truly be born evil or do you think it is created? Like do you think that little girl would have had a chance without Clayton in her life?"

Kenai thinks on that for a moment before answering. "Honestly, I'm not sure. I know there are some conditions, some actual neurological conditions, that make people do evil things, but I'd like to believe that all kids are born innocent."

"Me too," I say softly, tucking my legs up to my chest.

"How are you feeling? After seeing all that today?"

I shrug. "It was hard, but I feel mostly sympathy for that woman. The life she must have lived, I can't even imagine. The fear. No escape. I know what that monster was like. I know. I dealt with it for only a little while, she had years and years of torture. I'm so glad he's gone, and can't torture anyone else. Because honestly, can you imagine what he might have done to her?"

Kenai reaches over and squeezes my hand. "Yeah, it's a hard thing to imagine."

"She's at peace now, I just have to keep reminding myself of—"

Something launches out in front of the car. Kenai reacts quickly, slamming on the breaks and narrowly missing the dark object that darts off the other side of the road. My throat is tight and my body prickles with adrenaline as I watch it disappear into the darkness.

"Was that . . . was that a person?" I whisper, my voice failing me.

"I think so. Let me check it out. Stay here."

Kenai pulls the car over to the side of the road and then takes a flashlight from the center console and jumps out of the car, leaving it running. Fear prickles my skin and suddenly I'm finding it hard to breathe as everything goes black. I reach over to lock the door when movement outside catches my attention. I could swear I see a flash of red. Kaity? It couldn't be.

I don't think, I leap out of the car and call out, "Kaitlyn?"

Nothing.

I walk towards the back of the car, but no one seems to be anywhere near it. I squint into the trees, looking for Kenai, but I can't even see his flashlight anymore. "Kenai?" I call.

He doesn't speak.

Doesn't answer.

"Kenai?" I call again.

Still no answer.

The driver's door to the car slams shut, and I whip around just in time to see the reverse lights flick on. A loud squeal can be heard as the car starts speeding backwards towards me. I launch out of the way just in time, and then, with a spin of the wheels, the car takes off into the night. Someone just stole our car, after they tried to run me down. I brush off the dirt, my skin burning where it's been scratched.

"Kenai?" I scream into the darkness.

Nothing. Where is he?

I push to my feet and rush over in the direction he'd disappeared into. I shove into the trees, terrified, and see the faint glow of a flashlight on the ground. My heart races as I run forward, dropping to my knees beside it and picking it up. I shine it around and see Kenai bent over against a tree, clutching his stomach, struggling to breathe.

"Kenai!" I cry, rushing over.

He's got blood on his fingers.

No!

"Talk to me, tell me you're okay," I call frantically, shining the light on his stomach.

"Stabbed . . . me," he gasps. "Call an ambulance."

"Someone stole the car. Oh God. Kenai, don't panic, I'm going to find a way to help you."

"Struggling to breathe," he wheezes. "You need to get help, Marlie."

I close my eyes and try to think. I need to put pressure on his bleeding so he doesn't bleed to death before I can go to find any help. "Don't move too much, okay?" I say softly. "I need to control the bleeding."

He doesn't argue, he just carefully shifts until he's facing me. He removes his hand, which is covered in blood. His breathing is quite shallow, from panic or the wound I don't know. I hope panic. I pray panic. I gently lift his shirt, and like the alpha male he is, he doesn't make a sound. So strong. There is so much blood, it's hard to tell how deep or large the wound is.

"I can't tell much, but I'm going to put a little pressure on it so we can slow down this bleeding. Sit down, put your back against something so you're not trying to hold your weight up. Let your body rest."

I help him sit down against a tree, and he winces in pain as he lowers himself. I slide off my top and press it against his wound. He makes a throaty, pained sound and it kills me to know he's hurting, but I have to help him. "Put your hand on this, keep the pressure there. I'm going to call for help. Do you have your phone on you?"

"In the car."

"Mine too. I'll go out to the road, try to find help."

"Take the flashlight," he rasps.

"No, you need it. I'll be able to see once I get back out to the road."

He doesn't argue, and that scares me.

I tuck the flashlight between his legs, cup his

face gently, and then navigate my way back out onto the road. There isn't a car in sight, and I know we're a fair way out of town. I glance around, looking for something to remind me which direction I'm coming from, so I don't lose Kenai. There is a sign on the opposite side of the road that says something about a hotel a few miles ahead.

I take a mental picture, then I start walking in the direction it indicates. If I have to run a few miles, I will. I might be in my bra and pants, but I'm going to do this. Knees and pride be damned. I pick up into a jog, and get a few hundred feet down the road when I see car lights coming in my direction. I step off to the side of the road and start waving my arms around, but the car doesn't slow down. It takes me a moment to realize it's Kenai's rental car.

I launch off the side of the road, just as the car whizzes by me. It spins around, tires squealing, and my anger emerges. Kenai is hurt. Whoever this is—I'm tired of their game. I'm tired of being scared. I'm tired of running. I'm just so damned tired. The car speeds back towards me, and I roll once more, dodging its brutal attack.

No.

Not going to happen.

With a lump in my throat, but with a determination I've never felt, I pat my hands across the ground until I come up with a large, heavy rock. I clutch it with both hands, stand up, and start walking out onto the road. The car has just spun around again, and its lights are aimed at me, bright and deadly. I can't see who is behind the wheel but I can hear the engine rev. My heart feels like it's going to leap out of my throat.

"I'm not afraid of you anymore, you bitch!" I scream.

More revving.

"Do your best!" I scream. "You will not win this. You will not beat me."

I don't know if whoever is in that car can hear me, but I don't care.

The car hurtles towards me. I raise the rock in the air with all my strength. Whoever it is seems confident I'll leap out of the way. I don't. I stand right there in the middle of the road and when the car is close enough, I throw the rock with all my might then leap out of the way. The car swerves as the rock shatters the windshield, and suddenly it's spinning out of control. Tires screech as it hits the other side of the road then disappears into the trees.

I run towards it.

I'm tired of this.

I'm going to face my demons once and for all.

TWENTY

Smoke pours from the hood of the car, and the entire front end is smashed up and crushed against a tree. I reach down, pick up a stick, and clutch it close as I move to the driver's side door. My heart is in my throat, my hands are shaking, and my entire body is numb as I reach for the handle and jerk it open. I raise the stick, but the front seat is empty.

My eyes dart to the passenger side, then to the back.

Gone.

Whoever was in this car is now gone.

Devastation grips my chest and I press a hand over my heart, trying to control my breathing. So close, and yet so damned far.

Kenai.

I have to focus.

I rush around to the passenger side to find my purse, dig out my phone, and dial 911. I give the operator directions, then I rush back up onto the road and over the other side, heading towards the flashlight. Kenai is still propped against the tree, his head dropped, his hand pressed against his stomach.

"Hey," I say softly, dropping to my knees. "Kenai. Can you hear me?"

His eyes flicker open and his breathing is still ragged, but at least he's awake.

"What happened out there? I could hear it from here," he manages between rasping breaths.

"Whoever stole the car tried to run me down. I threw a rock through the windshield and they crashed. But they were gone before I could get to the car. Whoever it is, they're playing a dangerous game."

Kenai looks at me, and his lip twitches in a broken, pained attempt at a smile. "You threw a rock at the car?"

I grin. "Well, I'm tired of this game now. Whoever's doing this thinks I'm still the pathetic, weak Marlie. I'm not. I'm so much more."

He reaches out with a shaky, bloodied hand and runs his thumb down my cheek. "Fucking proud of you," he rasps.

"Stop talking, the ambulance is on its way. You're going to be fine, do you hear me?"

He nods and closes his eyes again.

I sit by him until I hear the familiar sirens whizzing down the road. I stand and rush out, waving them down. Then I stay clear as they get Kenai onto a stretcher and load him into the back. I climb in with him, holding his hand as we speed off into the night.

"You're Marlie Jacobson," the EMT officer says as we head towards the hospital.

I glance at him. He's not looking at me, but writing something on a sheet of paper. When I don't answer, he looks up.

"Sorry," he says, looking genuinely guilty.

"No, it's okay," I say. It's not his fault. "Yes, I am."

"I saw your story on the news. I used to work in Denver. I assisted when one of the other girls was, ah, found."

Oh.

"I'm sorry. That must have been awful."

I can only imagine how handling those bodies would have felt. Missing a scalp, tortured. I shiver.

"It was," he admits. "Which is why I admire you for your strength in getting out. I never read your book, but I saw what he did. You're a strong and brave person. It's truly an honor to meet you. If I had known I would be picking you up tonight, I would have dressed nicer."

He smiles.

I giggle.

"Stop hitting on my girl," Kenai rasps, squeezing my hand.

The EMT officer grins at me and I wink.

"You just rest," I order, stroking a finger down Kenai's face.

"I'm trying," he wheezes. "But it's really hard when he's trying to chat up my woman."

I roll my eyes and the EMT officer chuckles softly.

"I see you haven't lost your broodiness," I say, stroking Kanai's hair from his forehead. "Now stop talking and rest."

He grumbles.

But he does as he's told, for once in his life.

"He was very lucky, the knife just missed his lungs. Whoever stabbed him drove that blade intending to hit something vital. The angle came close to his left lung but fell just short," the doctor tells me early the next morning while Kenai is sleeping.

"That's good news," I sigh, exhausted.

"He should be able to go home tomorrow, but he'll need to take it easy. His wound is quite deep and he lost a good amount of blood."

"I understand. Thank you, Doctor."

I close my eyes when he leaves and rub my forehead.

Rest? Kenai?

That'll never happen with Kaity out there and me in danger. How is he going to find her when he's injured? Was this the plan all along? To take him out of the picture? I shudder at the thought and make my way towards his room, papers in my hand for us to go over. If he's stuck in this hospital another day, then we can at least figure out as much as we can about the situation.

I reach his room and peer in. He's propped up in the bed with his eyes closed, but I can see his fingers rubbing against his skin, so I know he's awake. I knock softly, and his eyes fly open and turn in my direction. I put up a hand and wave. "Hi there." I smile as I walk in and sit down on the end of his bed. "How're you feeling?"

"Not too bad. Pissed they won't let me get out of this hell hole."

I chuckle. "Typical male response."

He grunts. "Your sister is out there, Marlie. I don't want to be stuck in here when I could be out there helping her."

My chest clenches. "I know, I get it. I brought these," I say as I hold up the papers and the journal. "At least we can go over it all and try and see if there is anything to help us out as to the whereabouts of this daughter."

Kenai smiles weakly. "That's my girl, always thinking ahead."

I beam and hand him the bag of stuff he collected from the house. I flick open the diary and curl my legs beneath me, continuing to read the horrifying story of how Clayton's sister lived. It sends chills up my spine every time I open it. I hate reading the words and yet I find myself unable to stop.

Dear Diary,
She's getting worse.

Today she had a fit because I wouldn't let her go hunting with her father. She stormed into the kitchen and pulled out a knife, waving it around at me. I disappeared into the bedroom and locked the door, but I could hear her for hours, standing outside scraping the knife down the door, calling out to me, telling me I had to come out eventually.

I thought about going out and letting her end it.

I'm so tired.

But then he came home and stopped her. They went out for ice cream, as if they're just normal people who lead normal lives. I didn't complain. When they're gone, it's the only time I feel like I can breathe without fear gripping me. I should run. I should just pack up and leave.

But I know he'll find me.

Or she will.

I'm their prisoner for the rest of my life.

I flip the page and look up at Kenai, who is going over Clayton's case file again. He hasn't gone through the bag of things he collected. He looks up, and as his eyes meet mine he gives me a small smile and my heart pounds.

"Hi," he says softly.

"Hi yourself."

"Come over here, give me a kiss."

I put the diary down and get on my hands and knees, crawling towards him. When I reach him, I lean in and press my lips softly against his, trying not to put any pressure on him. We kiss for a long time, until we're distracted by my phone. I sigh and roll my eyes, pulling back and shuffling to the end of the bed so I can pick it up. It's Hannah.

"Hey, Han," I say, crossing my legs.

"Marlie! Hey! How's everything going?"

"It's getting there, a bit of a bump in the road, but it's nothing major."

"That sucks," she sympathizes. "Listen, are you still in San Diego?"

"Yeah, why is that?"

"I'm here!" she cries happily. "I was hoping you hadn't left yet. Do you want to grab a coffee?"

I smile. "I'd love that. When?"

"Today? Now, if you have time?"

I look to Kenai and cover the phone, saying, "Do you mind if I go and have a coffee with Hannah? She's in San Diego."

He shrugs. "Go for it. I need to sleep."

I beam. "I'm in," I say to Hannah. "Where do you want to meet?"

She gives me the name of a local coffee shop, and I promise to meet her there in half an hour. I hang up the phone and stand, gathering my things.

"Leave the diary, I'll keep going over this stuff while you're gone," Kenai says.

I nod, walking over and cupping his jaw, kissing him. "Are you going to be okay?"

He gives me a sour look.

I giggle.

"Of course you are, macho man. I forgot you don't need anyone."

He grunts.

"I'll be back in a few hours," I smile.

As I walk towards the door, Kenai calls my name. I stop and turn.

"Be careful, Marlie."

I smile. "Always."

TWENTY-ONE

KENAI

I watch her disappear out the door, and something squeezes deep in my chest. Something I've never felt before. I care about the girl who just walked out of my room more than I should in such a short time. The sharp pain in my gut has me shifting position, for the hundredth time today. I reach for the bag of items I collected from the little house. The sooner I can figure this out, the better.

I pull a couple of notes and books out first, flicking through them. There isn't much information, just bills and other such everyday matters. Grunting, I toss that stuff to the side and pull out a photo album. I open the dusty cover and stare down at the pictures. A lot of the house, some animals, some childhood photos of the two of them, a few of Clayton on his own, but there seems to be no pictures of their child. None at all. There are a few empty slots, and I wonder why those pictures have been removed.

Probably because the daughter is a deranged psychopath.

"Hi there."

I look up to see a young, blonde nurse coming into the room. I can see the blush in her cheeks from here.

"Hi," I mutter.

"I'm just doing a routine checkup, if you don't mind."

I shrug. "Whatever."

She laughs nervously as she checks me over, her fingers fumbling as she looks under my bandage. It's like the woman has never seen a man before. I keep quiet as she finishes up. When she's gone, I call the nurse's station and ask not to be disturbed for a few hours. It's crucial, now more than ever, that I get this psycho who's after Marlie and Kaitlyn. The danger is only going to get worse. I can feel it in my bones. I only wish I'd listened to Marlie sooner—then we might not be in this mess.

I feel like a fool for not believing her. I honestly thought she was just suffering paranoia from her ordeal. That made more sense in my mind than to actually believe that she could be right. What are the odds of it? I should have believed in her, and that's on me.

I jerk the bag back open and pull out some more items. I come across the purse I picked up from the table. I zip it open and flick through it. Some cash. A few old cards. Some receipts. I open those, most are just from food or alcohol purchases. I'm about to flip it closed when I notice a frayed edge sticking out of a tiny slot I hadn't noticed. I reach for it and pull out a photo. I look at the picture.

There is a little girl in it, and she seems familiar somehow. Maybe I've seen a photo somewhere of her? I try to recall it, but can't. I squint, bringing the picture closer. Where have I seen her before? She's a young, pretty blonde thing. Somewhat like the photos of what I'm assuming is her mother. I don't see why else this picture would be in here otherwise. I continue to study it, trying to place where I've seen that face.

Then I flip it over and my blood runs cold.

The name on the back.

No.

It can't be.

No.

I drop the picture and scramble for my phone, straining myself, my heart pounding as I get it into my hands and dial Marlie's number. A vibration is heard at the end of my bed and my eyes dart to her phone, tangled up in the blankets. It's vibrating. She must have dropped it. My heart races. No. Fuck. No.

I have to get to her.

I have to warn her.

My eyes move to the picture again and the scrawly, semi-faded writing on the back.

Hannah 1992.

TWENTY-TWO

MARLIE

"I've missed you!" I cry, hugging Hannah when she arrives at the coffee shop.

"Me too," she smiles, squeezing me. "I've been so worried."

She's such a good friend. Honestly, there are times I wonder how I'd have ever gotten through without her. One time in particular stands out. My heart warms recalling it.

I just can't do this anymore.

I'm curled on the bathroom floor. My head is in my hands and my body is trembling. Hannah has come over to see Kaity, but she isn't here. Somehow, somehow she knew to come in and check on me. I know the moment she enters the room, because I feel her arms go around me. I know they're hers. I can smell her familiar scent.

"It's going to be okay," she says softly.

"No," I whisper. "No, it feels like it'll never be okay again."

"It will. I promise. When all is said and done, you'll come out stronger."

"I don't know what I'm going to do. Or how I'm going to get through this."

"You're going to get through because you're strong. Because you're the strongest person I know. Believe that. Believe in yourself."

"I'll never not see his face. His awful, monstrous face."

She holds me closer. "There will come a time when all you see is yourself and your strength."

"It's been hard," I admit, snapping out of my memory, pointing to a table, where we sit down.

"I can imagine," she says, placing her hands out in front of her. She has scratches all over them.

"What happened to your hands?" I ask.

She stares down at them. "Oh, I was gardening. Got a bit excited. I could ask the same of you. What happened to your eye?"

I shrug. "It's been somewhat of an interesting trip."

"How so?" she asks, shifting in her seat.

She seems nervous.

She's probably as anxious as I am about Kaity.

"We found out Clayton had a daughter, who is a total psycho just like him. I think she has Kaity."

Her face tightens and she slams her hand on the table. "Why do you think that?"

"I found her mother's journal, and it turns out the little girl was as crazy as her father. It makes sense she'd want to avenge her dad. God knows why. That man deserved everything he got."

Hannah's phone rings, and she stares down at the screen, frowning. "Let me get this, Marlie."

She stands and disappears.

Something doesn't feel quite right.

I'm not sure what it is, but there is a warning in my chest, alerting my body that something isn't right. I glance around. Is the girl following me? Is she nearby? I study all the people surrounding our table, seeing if any of them are looking at me strangely, but they all seem to be minding their own business. Hannah returns a moment later, and she looks flustered.

"I'm sorry Marlie, I just got word my aunty who lives here has tripped in her home and needs some assistance."

"Oh no." I stand. "Do you need some help?"

She nods, a tear runs down her cheek. "Yes. I'm so worried. Would you mind? I'm sure you want to get back to Kenai."

"No, it's fine. Let's go."

We head to her rental car and climb in. I reach into my purse to let Kenai know where I'm going, but my phone isn't in my purse.

"Damn!" I mutter.

"What is it?" Hannah asks.

"I forgot my phone. Can I borrow yours to call Kenai?"

She frowns. "Sorry, the battery just went dead. Can you call him from my aunt's house?"

Crap.

"Never mind, we don't be long, right?"

She nods, driving off. "Right."

I wish I could get the feeling out of my chest screaming at me that something is wrong.

So very wrong.

TWENTY-THREE

KENAI

"Calm down, Kenai, I can't understand a fucking word you're saying," Darcy barks into the phone.

I'm slamming my finger on the nurse button over and over. Why the fuck hasn't one of them come in and checked on me? I could be fucking dying and they're dragging their damned feet.

"Kenai!" Darcy bellows and I jerk, removing my finger from the call button.

"I know who has Kaity and I'm certain she's just gotten ahold of Marlie, too. I'm stuck in this fucking hospital and she's in danger. I need you to get me the fuck out of here. We need to find her."

"Slow down. Who are you talking about?"

"Clayton had a fucking daughter, and that daughter has some sort of revenge plan, and Marlie is the target."

"I beg your pardon?"

"I don't have time to go over this with you. I need you to get everyone you know to help, Darcy. She's in danger, I can feel it in my fucking bones."

"Okay, give me all the information you have. Marlie have a phone we can track?"

"Would you believe she left it here?" I say, my chest tightening.

"That's fucking not good. Do you know where the two of them were last?"

I give him the name of the café Marlie said she was meeting Hannah at, as well as the address to Clayton's sister's house. With those things in his grasp, he promises me he'll get as many men as he can on it and call in a search.

"Get me out of here, Darcy."

"I can't do that, Kenai," he murmurs, his voice sympathetic. "You know I can't do that."

"She's in danger," I growl.

"Yeah and you're injured. What good are you to us or her?"

"I have information, I can help piece it together, I can help find her."

"No," he says firmly. "No you can't. I'll keep you updated. Sit tight. Call me if you find anything else."

"Darcy?" I say before he hangs up.

"Yeah?"

"Find my girl."

He exhales. "I'll do my best."

He hangs up the phone and I throw mine across the room, bellowing with rage. Marlie is in danger and I can do nothing but sit here and wait. I should've listened to her. That psycho bitch could be doing anything to her. She could be torturing her, or worse, and I'm worth nothing. I'm not able to provide one single thing. I can't protect her. I promised her she'd be safe with me, and I let her down.

For the second time in my life, my stupidity may cost someone I love the ultimate price.

TWENTY-FOUR

MARLIE

"I didn't know you had an aunt out here," I say to Hannah as we arrive at an old, run-down house in the woods. It's creepy. It's old. It makes me uneasy.

"Yeah," Hannah says, climbing out of the car. "She doesn't socialize much."

"Right," I mumble, getting out and following Hannah to the house. It seems familiar somehow.

As we walk up the rickety front steps, my stomach is flipping with anxiety. I can't shake the feeling something awful is about to happen. Maybe Hannah's aunt is dead in there. Oh God. What if that's what my bad feeling is about? I take a shaky breath and when Hannah opens the front door, I follow her inside.

The house is old and the floorboards creak. It's filled with dust, like it hasn't been lived in for a good, long while. If Hannah's aunt lives her, she's been living a hellish life, because I don't know how any human being could survive in here. It's awful. It smells and there are gigantic holes in the floor, showing the actual dirt beneath the house. I press a hand over my nose and glance around.

I don't see anyone.

In fact, it really looks like nobody has been here for years.

"Are you sure this is the right place?" I murmur, coughing from the dust.

I turn, but Hannah is nowhere to be seen. I glance down at her dusty footprints leading into the bedroom. She steps out a second later—with a shotgun in her hands.

"It's the right place," she says, her voice strange.

"Why have you got a gun?" I ask. "Is your aunt okay?"

She smiles, but it's the kind of smile that sends chills right through your bones. It's a cold, empty, emotionless smile.

"I don't have an aunty."

I blink.

My skin prickles.

"Sit down, Marlie."

I shake my head, confused. Is this a joke?

"What's going on, Han?"

She raises the gun and my blood runs cold. "I said sit down."

I'm confused. I don't know what's happening. I stumble backwards and my bottom falls down onto the dusty, old sofa behind me. Hannah keeps the gun raised. The evil smile on her face remains. Is this a joke? Hannah is my best friend. I don't understand.

"What's going on?" I say again, my voice shaky.

"I'm going to tell you a story," she says, lowering the gun and running her hands over it as she begins pacing the room.

"Hannah," I begin but she spins around.

"Shut up. If you speak, I'll shoot you."

I close my mouth as my body begins trembling. I'm starting to think my worst fears are about to present themselves.

"My story starts with a father. He was a great father. He spent so much time with me; he loved me; he let me be who I was. He understood my dark thoughts; he understood that I was different, because he was different, too. He was all I had."

I swallow.

Please no.

"He did some bad things, I know, but people didn't understand that it was part of him. They didn't understand because they didn't feel that intense need to kill like we did. It's in our DNA. It's wired deep. It's who we are. It's like a hunger you just can't contain. It doesn't matter how much you feed it, it'll never get better."

My hands tremble.

No.

NO.

"He was everything to me. When his life was

taken, it tormented me for so long. I knew I had to do something, I knew I had to get justice. I knew I had to finish what he started. It's what he would have wanted. He would want me to finish it. He would want me to let the world know that just because he's gone, doesn't mean he'll ever be forgotten. I'll never let him be forgotten. I'll make sure he gets what he deserves. I'll make sure you get what you deserve."

My vision blurs and horror flashes before me as reality slams in.

Hannah . . . my best friend, my trusted confidant, my beautiful Hannah . . .

"Y-Y-Y-Y-You're her," I whisper, my hands trembling. "You're his daughter."

She smiles wickedly. "Surprise."

I shake my head.

I can't believe it. I won't.

Hannah has been my friend since . . . since . . .

Since the start.

Oh God. I remember the first time we met. She was so . . . so . . . *real*.

"Marlie, this is my friend, Hannah," Kaity says.

I stare blankly at the girl my sister has brought in. I haven't spoken to many people since I've been home. I just haven't wanted to.

"Hi," Hannah says, then she surprises me by stepping forward and wrapping her arms around me. No one has been game to do that since I came home. "I'm so sorry for your ordeal. I hope you're okay."

The kindness in her eyes speaks volumes. She looks at me sincerely, as if willing to listen.

All I need is someone who will listen. I find myself warming to the stranger. The nonjudgmental, beautiful blonde stranger.

"Th-Th-Th-Thank you," *I stammer.*

"I don't know you, but my heart goes out to you. If you ever need to talk with someone, you can always talk with me."

With that, the stranger lets me go, and she and Kaity disappear down the hall.

And I know, I just know.

I've made a real friend.

"Was it all an act?" I say, rubbing my arms. "All of it . . . just an act?"

"I had to gain your trust. I couldn't have you doubt me even a little. And then you moved away, for years, and I tried to just move on but I couldn't." Her face goes red. "That book was everywhere. It wouldn't let me forget. You made my father look like a monster, and I knew I had to come up with a plan. I knew it would take time. I knew I had to be patient. So I befriended Kaity, the broken, lonely girl and then, through her, I got to you."

Tears well in my eyes. "We loved you."

She shrugs merrily. "Love bites, honey. Get used to it."

I shake my head again. "Why now?"

"I was tired of waiting. I couldn't get close enough to you without you getting suspicious, so when Kaity started running off the rails, I knew I could use her to bring you back to town. Then, I thought it would be fun to torment you a little. It's what my father would have wanted. And you know what? I loved every minute of it."

She laughs hysterically, like what she just said is so funny.

"Where is Kaity?" I dare to ask, my throat tightening.

"She's been with me the entire time. I needed her for the game."

The game.

"Your father is not the victim here," I dare to say, my eyes darting past her to see if I can find some way to escape.

I have no phone. I can't even call Kenai.

I should have listened to my instincts.

I should have listened.

"You killed him," she hisses, rubbing her hands over the gun.

Just like he used to.

How did I not notice the connection between them?

"He tried to kill me," I say carefully. "Just like he killed all those other girls."

"You wouldn't understand," she says, her eyes flashing. "The need, it's so strong. It's what we were sent here to do. It's our mission. We don't get a choice. All we know is that we crave the kill. He did nothing wrong. He was just being himself, and you"—she points the gun at me—"you ended him."

"He's a murderer," I say, trying to keep calm as I continue to study the room, searching for a way out.

But I have to get past her first.

I read a bit about deranged people after I was taken. I studied it. I wanted to understand how their minds worked, to a degree anyway. I wanted to know what made them tick. I often wondered if how I dealt with Clayton was the reason I got out. I saw the videos of the other girls. Some begged, some offered sexual favors, some just gave up, but I refused to break. Is that what saved me?

Is that what will save me now?

"He's not a murderer!" she screams. "You are."

Wrong tactic.

"We're friends, Hannah. Did none of that mean anything to you?"

She laughs. "You're delusional if you think anything mattered. It was an act. All an act."

"It wasn't for me," I say gently. "You're my best friend. I trust you. What we have, it matters to me. I'm sorry you feel your dad was taken from you, but you have to understand what he did was wrong, too."

He's a murderer.

A sick freak.

But I know, deep down in her mind, she doesn't believe that.

I have to play the game. I have to get out of here.

I won't live through this again.

"He didn't do anything wrong!" she hisses, twitching. "He couldn't help who he was."

"Neither can I."

Her eyes flash to mine.

"I was afraid. I didn't know that he, ah, was really a good person inside. I was just scared and had to get out. It was an accident really. I didn't mean to kill him."

The words feel like poison coming out of my mouth, they burn the same. Saying Clayton is a good person is like removing a tooth with a rusty instrument. But I'll say and do whatever I have to to get out of here, to change her mind, hell, to distract her for a few seconds so I can escape.

"You killed him. You drove a knife into his brain. You're a monster. You acted out of evil. He acted because he had no other choice."

"There is always a choice, Hannah. He didn't have to do that to those girls. He could have gotten help."

"You didn't have to kill him," she shrieks, pointing the gun at me. "You could have just done what he asked."

Let him scalp me?

Plan B isn't working so I change tack.

"Where's Kaitlyn?" I ask, diverting her attention to another subject.

Hannah is trembling.

She looks uneasy with the gun.

Her delusion frightens me.

It's as if she's an amateur. She's trying to be

something she was taught her whole life to be, but she isn't doing a good job. Maybe that's a good thing. Maybe her unease will be what helps us get out of here. As much as she wants to be, she's not like Clayton. She doesn't have the same cool, calm, and collected edge he had. Nothing bothered him. Nothing caused him to lose his focus. She's different.

"You'll find out when I decide to begin my game."

"Haven't you already been playing it?" I ask, staring at the front door.

"You run," she hisses, "I'll shoot you, Marlie."

I swallow, take a shaky breath, and look back to her.

"What if I don't want to play your game?"

She grins. It's sick, just like his.

"You simply don't get a choice."

Hannah is pacing, gun in her hand, mumbling to herself. She truly believes everything that psychotic man told her. While she paces, I look around for a way out. I could run, take the risk. She might hit me with that shotgun, but she might miss, too, if I move quickly, maybe zigzag. It's worth the risk, right? If I sit here, God knows what she's going to do to me.

I think about being locked away with Clayton.

I made a mistake, running into that closet.

Now I have a chance to get away, to do this right. I've learned a lot since then. I'm afraid, but dammit, I'm stronger. Hannah is smaller than me, and albeit crazy, she's still just a girl, and if there's any hope of getting through to her, that's the tool I can use. Emotions. Surely there has to be some in there, right?

"Your boyfriend will be freaking out by now, I can just imagine how hard he'll be taking it, not being able to chase after you," she says, chuckling to herself.

She's smart, I'll give her that much. Cutting Kenai out of the picture was a surefire way of making certain she could get to me. But why let me hire him in the first place?

"If you wanted him out of the picture," I say, deciding to keep her talking, "why did you push me to hire him in the first place?"

"As a tribute to my father. You see, the man thought to have killed Kenai's sister was someone my father hated, so he framed him. It was my father who killed the girl, taking her life and destroying an enemy in the process. It was quite genius, really. And equally genius of me to make him relive his sister's death all over again when I kill you. Can you imagine how powerless he'll feel? Blaming himself for allowing not just one, but two girls to be murdered on his watch. My father would be so proud."

I want to gauge her eyes out and shove them down her throat so she stops giggling.

"And as a bonus, I got to watch you fight while

you drove halfway across the country, you terrified, while I had your sister the whole time. It was entertaining. I won't lie. Especially when I paid those men to taunt you at the club. You fell for everything, hook, line, and sinker. I wondered how long it would take you to figure out you were being duped. I can't believe you made it all the way to Los Angeles before figuring it out. It's sad, really. You both failed."

"I knew," I mutter. "Deep in my gut. I just didn't want to believe it."

"Maybe if you did, we wouldn't be here. I guess my father taught you nothing."

"Unlike you. It looks like he taught you all of his secrets," I say, hoping flattery gets her to lower her defenses. I take in the gun she's holding.

It's a gun.

Not easy to fire a shot quickly.

If I lunge for it, she'd have a clear shot at me. It would be better to run. The second I got outside, I could run into the woods, zigzag through trees, and she'd not be able to catch me easily.

It seems like the best option. The longer I stay here, the greater my chances of being killed.

"It was all a lesson!" she barks. "All of it."

"Enlighten me, then," I say, watching as she begins to pace again.

I won't get many more chances.

The front door is about four feet away. Then I have to get it open.

"He had a purpose," she begins, and when she turns her back to the front door and starts pacing in the opposite direction, I make my move.

I launch out of the chair and run towards the door. I hear her turn, scream at me, and then the gun goes off. A bullet whizzes right past my thigh and my heart leaps into my throat. I reach the front door and shove it open, throwing myself out and dropping low. As I surge forward, another bullet whizzes by, the crack of the shotgun filling the air.

I tumble down the front steps, shove to my feet—pain and all—and I run. I zigzag as I do, praying it's enough. I saw it on a self-defense show once. Hannah starts laughing hysterically, and for a moment, I wonder what the hell she's laughing at. I don't look back and check, I just keep running. I run past her car, wondering why she hasn't shot at me again.

Then I step into the woods and an explosion comes out of nowhere, throwing me backwards. I fly so far and hit the ground so hard, I hear my wrist snap on impact. My screams fill the woods as my face slides across the dirt, my body still travelling from the force of the explosion. My ribs scream in agony as my body twists in pain.

Hannah's laugh fills the air.

Evil.

Deranged.

I underestimated her.

She storms over, and I want to get up and run,

but I can't. I can't move. The pain in my wrist is like a fire has taken hold of my arm, I know I've broken at least three of my fingers, and my ribs feel like a hundred-pound weight is sitting on them. My body burns all over from the impact, and I can see blood trickling down my legs. Hannah reaches me, leans down, and curls her fist into my hair, screaming, "Get up. You stupid, foolish girl. Do you honestly think you can escape me?"

She starts pulling, and my scalp burns as my hair starts to dislodge. Memories of Clayton fill my head, and for a moment my body goes numb. I'm forced to move as she pulls, to save my hair from being torn out. My body flails as I try to scurry across the dirt after her. She's got a strong grip and she's pulling with all her might.

"The world thinks you're the smart one, that you were cunning enough to get away from my dad."

Tears burn under my eyelids as she drags me to the front steps.

"You're not so smart now, are you, Marlie? This whole thing has been amazingly easy."

She giggles to herself as she jerks me up the stairs.

"I thought you'd make this game fun for me, but Kaitlyn has made it more entertaining thus far."

I force my body up the stairs behind her. She kicks the front door open and my scalp feels like someone has poured acid over it, she's pulling so hard. She drags me down the hall to a room that's fully secured with a lockable pad on the outside. Just like his. She punches in a code, and then kicks the door open.

It's then that I see her.

My sister.

My baby sister.

No.

Kaity.

No.

TWENTY-FIVE

KENAI

I stand, ripping the drip from my arm. The nurse makes a frustrated sound and storms over. "Mr. Michelson, you can't do that."

"Do you have a legal right to keep me here?" I snap.

She crosses her arms. "No, but if you injure yourself . . ."

"Then that's on me."

She goes red in the face, but turns and disappears. I find my clothes and painfully jerk them on. My wound burns, but my heart, my fucking heart, is killing me. I need to get to her. Dammit. I should have known. I should have trusted my instincts but I didn't. I let her go out there on her own. I let her go knowing there was danger lurking.

I'll never forgive myself for that.

"What the hell do you think you're doing?" Darcy mutters, appearing in my doorway.

"Getting out. I'm not waiting any longer. I can help, Darcy, and you know it."

"You killing yourself on my watch isn't something I'm willing to sign on to. Get back into bed, Kenai."

"I'll fight you," I growl. "Do you understand me? I will go down bleeding, but I will fight you, Darcy. I need to go to her. Not one single thing you say or do will stop me. So you can either help me or you can get the fuck out of my way."

He studies me. "Dammit. You're serious."

"She's my girl. Of course I'm fucking serious."

He sighs. "I'll get you where you need to go, Kenai, but I'm telling you right now you're not doing any physical stuff. I'll let you help with tracking them down, but that's it. If you can't agree, I'll leave your ass here and have an escort at your door to make sure you don't get out."

I glare at him. He crosses his arms and stares at me. He's not going to back down. Of course he isn't.

"Fine," I grumble.

"Right. I'll go and talk to that poor flustered nurse while you think about every bit of information you know. Time is crucial. We can't mess around with this. Those girls are in danger."

I know they are.
And I'm terrified.

MARLIE

"Kaity," I cry, dropping to my knees, ignoring the pain that travels through my body.

My sister is almost lifeless on the ground. For a few agonizing seconds, I thought she was dead until I saw the faint rise and fall of her chest. My heart burns for her—it feels like a fist is closed around it and it's being ripped out of my chest. Slowly. Her body is frail and weak, her hair is cut off in chunks. Only pieces of her beautiful red locks remain. She has bruises and cuts all over her body. Her hands are bloody. Her wrists are red raw. Her left leg is swollen.

My poor sister has been tortured.

I didn't find her in time.

I carefully lift her head with my good hand. My wrist feels like someone is hacking it off with a blunt instrument, and I'm panting and sweating in pain. My fingers are swollen up like balloons. I don't care, though. This is my sister. My baby sister. She needs me. I'll endure any pain in this world to make sure she gets out of here safely. She's suffered enough because of my ordeal. I place her head in my lap and stroke a hand over her face. "Kaity, wake up. Please wake up and let me know it's not too late."

She stirs and her eyelids flutter open. Bloodshot blue eyes stare up at me. "Marlie?" she croaks.

"It's me. I'm here. I'm so sorry Kaity. So sorry. I never should have let this happen. Are you okay? Tell me you're okay."

"Everything hurts," she whispers.

"I know honey, I know it does. I'm going to get us out of here. I promise you."

"It's H-H-H-H-Hannah."

"I know," I say, stroking the chunks of hair away from her forehead. "I know sweetheart."

"She was my best friend," she sobs, but no tears run down her face. "She was my best friend and I trusted her. It's my fault. I should have never let her in. I should have known."

"There is no way you could have known, Kaity. None. This isn't your fault. It's mine. She wants revenge, and she used you to get to me, but I promise you I'll get us out of here."

She shakes her head and winces in pain. "She has everything covered. She's going to end this, Marlie. For him. We're not escaping. I've tried all of it. She has a plan for everything."

"Do not give up hope until you take your last breath, Kaity. There is *always* a way out. There is *always* a weakness. We just have to find it."

She shakes her head, but I press my hand to her forehead and gently stop her. "Trust me, I've been in this position. I know how terrifying it is, but I'm going to make sure we fight until there is no fight left. And Kenai won't let anything happen to me, or you. He'll be looking for us. We're going to get out of here."

"Kenai Michaelson?" she whispers.

"I hired him to help me find you. Hannah led me to believe you were involved with drugs and brought Kenai in so she could hurt him too. I'm so sorry. I should have known from the start."

"She's smart," she says hoarsely. "You would have never figured it out. She was my best friend and I had no idea."

The door alarm pings and both Kaity and I look over to see Hannah coming in with a bag in her hand. "Ah. I see we've had our reunion," she sings, closing and locking the door behind her.

Neither of us says anything.

"It's okay," she continues. "You don't have to speak. I'm going to do all of the talking anyway."

She walks over as if we're having some sort of slumber party and sits cross-legged on the old bed. "So, you know my dad had a fetish for hair. It was his thing. He used to brush my hair for hours when I was a little girl. He told me I have the prettiest hair. I do, don't you think?"

We both stare at her.

She giggles and continues.

"Anyway, he wanted a collection. All the colors. Like a hairdresser, you know? It's like, you can pick which color you want."

My stomach turns, but I don't show any reaction.

"Then you killed him," she says, glaring at me. "And you ended his life before he could reach his goal. You ruined it for him."

"He ruined it for himself," Kaity croaks. "He

could have just taken a lock of hair. Instead he scalped and killed them. He's a murderer. A sick, dirty bastard."

I squeeze Kaity's hand softly, to try to stop her from talking, but Hannah's face has already turned an ugly shade of red. That would explain why Kaity is in such a bad way. She's been stirring Hannah.

"I'll scalp you for no good reason, just for saying that," Hannah yells, fists clenching.

"You've already started it," Kaity hisses. "Might as well finish it."

"Kaity," I say, squeezing her again. "Don't."

"Listen to your sister, Kaity," Hannah says through clenched teeth. "She knows. She's smarter than you."

Kaity closes her mouth, but the look on her face is murderous. There is also a hint of betrayal there. Maybe even a little hurt. I can't say I blame her. I can only imagine the shock when she found out Hannah was the one behind all of this. It was hard enough for me, but Hannah was Kaity's rock. She truly believed in her. She loved her. She trusted her.

"Now, what I was saying before I was so rudely interrupted, was that I'm going to finish my father's game. Finish his collection. Starting with you, Marlie. Considering you took it all from him, I need to make it the most painful for you. The most drawn out. I read all his notes. I know what has to be done. But first, we need to fix these poor, faded scalps and get them fixed up."

She lifts a bag off the floor and tosses it on the bed. The police were never able to find them, yet here they are. A pile of old, decayed scalps fly out, and vomit rises in my throat. I remember everything from my time with that monster as I study the faded, ratty locks of hair on the bed.

Keep it together, Marlie. She wants to break you.

He didn't win. She won't either.

I take a shaky breath, steel my features and look up at her. "How pathetic. You can't even get your own hair, so you have to reuse these old, dirty ones."

Hannah's face flashes and she bares her teeth. "Don't push me, Marlie."

I glare at her.

"You and Kaity are going to wash, dry, and straighten these. Make them look good as new. Then you're going to hang them over there."

She points to the wall and I stare at it. It's blank. There's nothing on it.

"I'm hanging some hooks, and you two are going to help me finish the collection. Then, I'm going to give my father the grand finale he deserved, by taking the scalp of the one who got away."

Her eyes flicker to me.

My stomach twists, but I control my disgust. She will not see me weak.

"Oh, there's one more thing."

She stands then disappears out of the room for a few minutes, locking the door behind her. Kaity and I stare at the scalps on the bed, and Kaity whispers, "I never understood it, Marlie. I could never truly fathom how it must have felt. But now, now I'm starting to understand the horror you lived through."

I squeeze her hand. My wrist is pounding. My fingers are beyond painful. My stomach hurts from the pain. I know I'm probably not strong enough to overpower Hannah, but dammit, I'll find a way out of this. "We're going to get out of here, I promise. Just do one thing for me, keep your mouth closed and trust me. I'll get us out, but I need you to let me talk."

Kaity nods. "Okay," she whispers. "Marlie?"

"Yeah?"

"I don't want to touch those."

I look to the scalps. "I know, honey. I know."

The door swings open and Hannah enters again, only this time she's not alone. A small, fragile girl is bound and gagged in her grips. She couldn't be any older than eighteen, maybe nineteen. She has the most incredible-colored hair. I've never seen anything quite like it. It's so blonde that it almost has a silvery tinge. Like a damned angel's hair. It's the most beautiful hair I've ever seen.

"I decided," Hannah says, tossing the girl in, "I was going to finish my father's collection with the most unique colors I could find. Yasmin here is the first on that list. I picked her up a few days ago." She shoves Yasmin in and she stumbles forward, not being able to catch herself because her hands are bound. She falls facefirst onto the ground and squirms. Poor girl.

"Now," Hannah continues. "Get acquainted with her. Because you two are going to be removing that gorgeous hair for my first masterpiece. I can't wait to watch. Won't that be fun?"

My stomach twists.

Kaity gags.

Yasmin whimpers.

"Us?" Kaity squeaks.

"Yes, you. Now, clean those scalps. Tomorrow, the fun begins. I'm so excited!" She claps happily, then disappears out of the room again.

I carefully let Kaity go and climb down to help Yasmin up. I untie her hands and remove the gag from her mouth. Poor girl is terrified.

"I'm Marlie, and this is Kaity. Please don't worry. I'll get us out of here."

"I'm so afraid," she whispers, her voice so soft.

"It'll be okay," I say, glancing at the door.

I hope.

TWENTY-SIX

Hannah returns with big tubs of water, shampoos, conditioners, creams, and oils, as well as brushes, hair dryers, and straighteners. I say nothing as I take in the straighteners. Those generate heat, a good amount of heat. She's giving us a weapon, even if she doesn't realize it. She requests that we have them all cleaned and dried within two hours, because she has a surprise for us later.

Nobody argues.

She's delusional and we need to keep her from hurting us as long as possible.

She locks the door, and we all stare at the scalps on the bed. Nobody wants to have to do this, but it's starting to look like we won't get a choice. Yasmin has been sobbing on and off. In addition to being terrified, she appears to have broken fingers, too. I don't ask how Hannah did it, but I suspect it was the work of her father's baseball bat.

Kaity has fallen silent, her body worn and tired. It's up to me to get these girls out of here, but right now I just don't know how I'm going to do that. Hannah has a weakness. I just need to figure out what it is.

I take the job of washing the scalps. The other girls find it too difficult. Somewhere inside me I muster up the strength, swallow down my horror and pain, and I wash them. I dry them, I straighten them, and then I put them back in the bag so I don't ever have to look at them again. As I'm stuffing the last, brown-haired scalp into the bag, it hits me.

Clayton.

Hannah's weakness is Clayton.

If it weren't for him, she would have never done what she's doing. If she didn't want to make him proud of her, because she loved him so much, she wouldn't be here. That's her weakness. Finishing the game. Making it perfect for him. If I make her doubt herself, if I weaken her and throw her off, we might just be able to find a way out of here.

It's a risk, though.

But it seems like my best option. A plan starts to take shape. I turn to the girls and whisper, "Listen, I need you two to do something for me."

They both look to me, eyes wide, maybe even hopeful.

"What's that?" Kaity asks.

"I need you both to let me do my thing here. I know that isn't going to be easy, and Hannah may react in such a way that you'll want to help me, but I'm begging you to trust me and not do anything. Even if she hurts me."

"Marlie," Kaity begins, but I cut her off by putting up a hand.

"No, you need to trust me. I know Hannah's weak point, I'm the one she wants. You need to believe in me, and let me do this. It'll be the only chance we have of getting out alive."

They both look wearily at me.

"Please," I say softly. "Just let me do this. I'll get us out of here."

They both nod, hesitantly.

"When you get the chance, and I'll make sure you do, run. Don't look back. Don't wait for me. Just run. Go and get help. Promise me you'll do that."

Yasmin nods. Kaity hesitates. I shuffle over to her and take her hands. "Promise me, Kaity. I need to know you'll do as I'm asking."

She holds my eyes, then she nods.

"I love you," I whisper.

"I love you too."

The door swings open and we all turn to see Hannah strolling in. She's got a bunch of dead squirrels in her hands. She's holding them upside down, and she has a massive grin on her face. "Hello, my pretties. I have wonderful news. It's time to start practicing. I can't have you ruining my work because you do a terrible job. My dad and I used to skin squirrels all the time, he taught me how to do it. Now I'm going to teach you."

I snort.

Her eyes flick to me. "Have you got a problem, Marlie?"

"Not at all," I say. "It just seems . . . never mind."

She drops the squirrels to the floor. "What?"

"I just think Clayton would have taught you a little better than that. He was so skilled at what he did. So precise. Squirrels seems . . . well . . . amateurish."

Hannah's eyes flare, and I know I'm right. I know that her father is indeed her weakness.

"He'd be proud of me. He taught me this. You know nothing. Now shut up and do as I'm saying."

"Whatever," I mumble beneath my breath.

She lifts her shirt and pulls a massive knife from her pants. The sight of the blade is so familiar, and my stomach turns when I realize it's the same kind of knife Clayton used in the videos he made me watch. Hannah runs her fingers over the sharp edge. "Who's going to go first?"

"No," Yasmin whimpers.

I glance at her, and her face is ghostly white. I know how terrified she is. But if she freaks out, and Hannah is indeed anything like her father, she'll make her suffer.

"It'll be okay," I say to her, trying to catch her

attention, but she's staring at the squirrels with horror in her eyes.

"I think Yasmin can go first," Hannah chirps, stepping forward and pulling another small carving knife from her pants. She hands it to Yasmin.

Yasmin stares at it.

"I'll go first," I say, but Hannah points her knife at me, stopping me when I try to step forward.

"I said Yasmin will go first," she says, her eyes turning cold.

"I don't want to," Yasmin wails. "No. I won't do it."

Hannah turns back to her.

"Yasmin," I try again, but she's got tears running down her cheeks.

She's going to freak out.

I can see it coming.

"Yasmin!" I try again. "Please."

She leaps to her feet and stumbles backwards, then she makes the fatal mistake of trying to scurry past Hannah.

Hannah steps in front of her, and drives the knife into Yasmin's arm. The sickening squelch has my stomach turning and Kaity making a pained, whimpering sound beside me. Yasmin stumbles backwards, and blood pours from her arm as she starts to scream.

"Stop your screaming!" Hannah yells. "Or I'll cut your fingers off."

"Let me go," Yasmin sobs, her hand covered in

blood as she clutches her arm. It's deep. I can tell that from here. "Let me go."

Hannah steps forward again and raises the knife.

I have to think fast. The door is locked and I don't trust our ability to fight Hannah in the states we're in. So I do the opposite. I laugh.

Hannah stops, her body going stiff.

She turns towards me. "What are you laughing at?"

I press my good hand to my mouth, as if trying to smother it. If only she knew inside, my heart was pounding so hard it feels like I'm going to pass out.

"It's just you think you're like Clayton, but you're not. He was so in control. So calm. So collected. He didn't need to raise a knife and stab people randomly to get his way. Hurting them was an absolute last resort. I'm sure he'd be rolling in his grave if he could see how pathetic you look right now."

Blood rushes to her cheeks and her eyes flash with hurt, before turning into red-hot anger. She storms towards me, leaning down and picking up a squirrel on her way. "Don't you dare tell me I'm not as good as him. He taught me everything I know. I'm making him proud. You shut up."

I keep my hand over my mouth.

She shoves the squirrel at me. "Skin it. Now."

"No."

Her eyes flare, and her fingers tremble around the knife.

"Now, Marlie. Or I'll—"

"What?" I cut her off. "You'll stab me? You'll chop my finger off? What? What are you going to do, Hannah? You're making your father ashamed. Hell, *I'm* ashamed."

She flinches, and then she lunges forward.

She lands on top of me, taking my hair in her hands and jerking my head back. My scalp burns, but I don't fight her. I just pray I'm on the right path. Kaity whimpers, Yasmin sobs, but as promised, neither of them interrupt. Hannah presses the knife to my throat, and I can feel the blade cutting into my skin. The burn radiates through my throat.

"I could slit your throat and make them watch you bleed out."

"Do it," I snarl.

Her hand shakes.

I feel like I'm going to pass out from fear, but I don't let it show.

"Well," I yell in her face. "Do it. Ruin all your father's plans. You're doing a fine job of screwing them all up right now, you might as well add to it."

Her hand continues to tremble.

Then she shoves off me and charges out of the room, hastily locking the door once it slams.

The carving knife is still on the ground.

She fucked up.

My plan worked.

"I know it hurts," I say softly to Yasmin.

I tear the sheet off the bed and use the carving knife to cut a piece off to wrap around her arm. I was right, the wound is deep and it's nasty. Her fingers are so swollen they're painful to look at. But there is little I can do for her in here. I know. I feel the same pain in my own fingers. I have to focus on getting us out. To do that, I have to enrage Hannah. I have to make her lose it. I have to distract her long enough for these two girls to run. The only way I can do that is to do something extreme. Something that'll make her flip her lid.

"How are we going to run, Marlie?" Kaity says, looking weaker by the minute. "She has those explosives around the house. She would come in here and tell me all about them so I wouldn't try and escape."

"I could be wrong, but I set those explosives off and I don't think that she's had time to replant them all. I think you should be safe, but you'll see them. If you're looking for them, you'll see them. She'll have a line set up. You step over it. Then you run. If you see any kind of weapons, you take them. If, for some reason, you can't get out through the door or a window, you find a weapon and hide together. Yasmin's hands are no good, so Kaity, it'll be up to you to keep Yasmin safe. Again, if you can't get out of the house, you hide and you don't move until you know it's safe. She'll be focused on me. I'm her priority. If anything happens to me, you need to take her by surprise and attack. Understand?"

Kaity nods.

"I know you're weakened, but you have to find your strength to get out of here or you'll never get away. Promise me you'll do that. Promise me you'll do anything you can, that you'll fight strong, to get out of here and to make sure Yasmin gets out too."

Kaity nods again. "I'll fight."

I smile.

"Please don't get hurt, Marlie. I can't live without you. I don't want to lose you."

"Trust me," I say, smiling even though my insides are screaming with fear. "I know what I'm doing."

Do I?

God, I hope so.

"So what's the plan?" Kaity asks as Yasmin whimpers again in the corner of the bed, clutching her arm.

"I'm not going to use the knife to attack her, I'm going to use it taunt her. She's going to come in here, and I'm going to be standing at the door with the scalps and the knife. I'm going to cut them. If I have read her right, losing the scalps her dad worked so hard for will destroy her. I'm hoping she'll be so distracted by it she won't shut the door behind her. You two run. And don't look back."

Kaity nods.

I look to Yasmin.

She nods, too.

I stand and walk over to the bag of scalps Hannah didn't take after her last exit. I lift them out, cringing. I hold the hair part in my hand, so I can hang on to all of them. That's the part they love the most. That's the prized part. Hannah will do just about anything to protect the hair. I'm sure of it. I hold the hair in one hand, and the carving knife in the other.

Then I stand by the door, just far enough back for it to be able to open without hitting me. Kaity and Yasmin sit to my left, both of them holding hands, both of them ready to run.

Now I wait.

And pray to God this works.

TWENTY-SEVEN

It feels like I stand at that door for hours. My legs ache. My knees hurt. My wrist burns. My fingers throb. But I don't move. I stare at it, just waiting for it to open. After a while, it does. For a second, Hannah doesn't enter, and I wonder if she's heard our plans, but then I realize she's pushing the door wide open so she can wheel a television in. She's going to play movies. I know exactly what kind of movies she's going to play.

I've seen them all before.

But it works out for the best, because she's had to open the door wide to get the television through. She turns just before she wheels it in, and her eyes catch sight of me with the hair and the knife. She freezes as all the color drains from her face. The exact reaction I wanted. I don't focus on Kaity and Yasmin, I just take a few shaky steps backwards.

"What are you doing?" Hannah says. "Put those down. Now."

"No," I say. "No. I'm not playing your sick little game anymore. It's time to destroy these."

Her eyes flare and she takes a step towards me, not once glancing at Kaity and Yasmin. She's leaving the door wide open for them.

"Don't," Hannah says, her voice cracking. "Don't you touch those. They're his. They're not yours."

"That's exactly why it's time they got destroyed. Your game is over, Hannah."

She takes a step and I press the knife to the hair, cutting enough so that a strand falls to the ground.

"No!" she shrieks. "Don't. Don't cut those."

I slice off another piece.

"Marlie!" Hannah cries. "Stop. Don't do that. Don't cut his hair. Don't touch those. Don't."

I see Kaity and Yasmin move slowly towards the door. A few more seconds and they're out.

Holding the scalps, I cut the hair again. "He really loved these. Imagine how disappointed he'd be that you let them be destroyed because you're so careless. You think you're good enough to continue his game, but you're not. You're not good enough. He'd be so disappointed in you, Hannah."

As I slice another piece, she lunges at me. Kaity and Yasmin disappear out the door. They're safe. Thank God. My relief disappears when Hannah lands on me. I lost my concentration for a second, and now I'm toppling backwards and she's making a grab for the hair. I hit the ground hard, and my wrist twists beneath me, causing me to scream out in pain. Hannah takes the hair and rolls off me, clutching the scalps to her chest, her eyes frantic as her fingers run over them.

"You ruined them!" She screams.

I push up, as pain explodes up my arm. I reach for the carving knife, but Hannah finally realizes what's happened. Her eyes dart to the door, to the empty room, and to my hand.

"You little bitch!"

She lunges for the knife, getting to it quicker than I do. She drives it into my broken finger, pinning it to the ground. I scream out in agony and automatically pull back, only to drive it deeper. My screams turn to strangled sobs as I try to free my finger. "I'm going to make you wish you were never born," Hannah snarls. "You're going to suffer for letting them go. I'm going to torture you for ruining my dad's hard work. Fuck you, Marlie."

She jerks the knife from my finger, pulls out her massive hunting knife, and stands, curling her fingers into my hair and jerking me to my feet by pulling so hard I have to get up. She drags me out of the room and into the living area. She pulls me over to the table and barks, "I'll stop your pathetic escape attempts. You say I'm not as good as my dad. Why do you think he cut those girls fingers off? How many doors can you open with no fingers?"

Oh God.

I never looked at it like that.

"Put your hand on the table."

I whip my head around. "No."

"Put it on the table!" She screams, jerking my head back by my hair so hard I feel a chunk dislodge.

"No!" I scream.

She releases my hair and raises the knife.

I take the moment to duck.

She swings it into nothing.

I hit the ground on my knees and scurry forward under the table. She moves quickly, reaching down and capturing my ankle. She jerks me backwards, and I fall onto my stomach. Pain. So much pain. Both my hands are on fire, but I don't let it stop me. I kick and squirm.

A sharp burning pain drives into my calf.

She just stabbed me.

I scream and kick out, connecting with something. A loud crack fills the room and I hear a thump as she hits the floor. Through the burning fire in my hands, I keep pushing myself forward until I get out the other side of the table. I push to my feet, gagging from the incredible agony, and I run towards the back door.

"No!" Hannah shrieks.

I shove it open and practically throw myself off the patio. It's getting dark. The afternoon is about ready to make its exit for the evening to come in. My stomach twists as I hobble-run towards the trees. I trip on a rock, slowing myself down. I can hear Hannah behind me. Her footsteps pounding across the dirt.

"You want a chase!" she screams. "I'll hunt you down like the animal you are, Marlie Jacobson."

TWENTY-EIGHT

KENAI

"Dammit!" I roar, sending my fist flying into the car door.

"Calm down, Kenai," Darcy barks. "We're moving as fast as we can. We can't hurry this up. You know we're trying."

"She's out there, she could be dead, and we've got nothing. We can't find a single piece of information on this girl and where she might be hiding them."

"We'll find her."

"It'll be too late!" I roar.

We arrive at the hotel and I launch out of the truck, ignoring the pain in my guts as I storm inside. Darcy follows. We've been looking all day. Night has fallen. It's been nearly two days. We have nothing. Not a single fucking thing. We have no idea where Hannah is keeping the girls or what she's doing to them.

If we don't find them soon . . . God only knows what she'll do to them.

I'm the best tracker I know, but I don't even know where to fucking look.

I'm so stressed, I can think only of Marlie. I can't think of anything else. I can't work. I just keep thinking of her beautiful face, wondering how the hell she's going to make it through this again.

It's my damned fault.

I should have listened to her.

"Yeah?"

I turn to see Darcy pressing the phone to his ear.

"What did you say?" he yells, about to drop his keys on the table. He doesn't drop them though. "When?"

He becomes a blur as he charges back towards the front door. "We're coming."

He hangs up and turns to me. "Marlie's sister just arrived at the police station with another girl. They escaped."

"What?" I yell, rushing towards him. "Marlie?"

"Not with them. Let's go."

Fuck.

We run back out to the truck, and Darcy races the entire way to the station. He hasn't even stopped the car before I am out of it and running inside, pain be damned. "Kenai!" he calls after me, but I don't stop.

I move through the front doors and straight to the reception desk. "Where is Kaitlyn Jacobson?"

"She's being questioned right now," the receptionist says. "She—"

I turn and charge down the hall.

"Sir!" The girl calls. "You can't go down there."

I find the interrogation room and shove the door open, bursting in. Kaitlyn and another girl are sitting, each wrapped in a towel, being looked at by paramedics. I skid to a stop when I take them in. Kaitlyn is in a bad way. Bruised and battered, she looks exhausted, tired, hungry. Her eyes swing to me when I enter and she whispers, "Are you Kenai?"

I nod, rushing in.

I kneel in front of her. "Where's Marlie?"

"She . . . she got us out. She told us to come and get help. I'm scared, Kenai. Hannah will kill her."

My girl made sure they got out alive.

God.

My beautiful girl.

"Where are they?"

"I . . . I don't know exactly how to get there, but wh-wh-wh-when we got out and ran, we found a road and a nice woman brought us into the police station. She's still here. She'll know the road. If you have her take you back, you'll see a dirt track, go down it. There is an old shack. They're in there. Hurry, Kenai. Marlie is hurt."

Marlie is hurt.

My vision swims.

I cup Kaity's face. "I'll find her. I promise you."

TWENTY-NINE

MARLIE

I fall to my knees, my body exhausted. I can't run anymore.

Everything blurs as I try to stop myself from passing out on the spot. My lungs burn as I scramble for air and try to push my body up.

She's right behind me.

Any second she'll appear.

Like a rabid dog, she just won't stop.

The sun is dropping lower and lower with every passing minute. I'm praying for nightfall. Praying for the darkness to help me escape. To help me hide. If she gets to me before the darkness falls, I know she'll kill me. She'll take my life without hesitation now. She's enraged. She's desperate. She'll do whatever it takes.

"I know you're out here, Marlie," she calls through the trees.

I push my back against a trunk, trying to catch my breath. Praying the tree is big enough to hide me.

"I'm going to make this painful. I'm going to end you just like Daddy should have. You never gave him the chance. You killed him. Now I'm going to kill you. An eye for an eye. I wanted to honor him, but now I just want you dead. I'll start over. I'll honor his legacy."

I try to slow down my breathing, so she won't hear it, but it's nearly impossible.

"I know you're here, nobody can run with knees like yours."

I scramble around, looking for something heavy. I find a large, thick branch and I lunge forward, lifting it up with my good hand. Even that one is badly battered, and pain shoots up my arm, but I take a deep breath and work through it. Hannah rounds the tree, a wicked smile on her face.

I swing.

The branch hits her right in the knees.

I swing again.

Her screams echo through the trees as a sickening crunch fills the quiet space. She drops down to the ground, and the heaviness of the branch weighs on me. I can't lift it again. So instead I drop it, shoving to my feet and running.

"I'll kill you," she wails in agony. "I'll kill you."

I drag my broken body over a few branches and start trying to fight my way through the trees again. My vision continues to blur as I try to escape.

I have to end this. Somehow I have to end this.

Hannah has found her way to her feet again, and is hobbling after me, screeching profanities. If she gets hold of me, she's going to make me suffer. One of us is going die tonight. If I don't do something, it's going to be me. I got away once. Dammit, I'm going to get away again.

A knife hurtles through the air and catches hold of my shirt, driving it into a tree. Holy shit. She has skill. I guess Clayton did teach her something. Frantically, I try to pull the knife from the tree, or at least dislodge my shirt, but it slows me down too much. A fist curls into my hair and pain explodes in the back of my head.

She's trying to scalp me.

A pain I never thought I'd ever feel again courses through me. It burns in the back of my head and warm blood trickles down my neck. No.

No.

I won't die like this.

I drive my elbow backwards, stunning her enough for her to release my hair for a second. Blood soaks my shirt as I spin around, tearing my shirt from the knife and the tree. Hannah lunges at me, bloodied knife in her hands. She hits me and we crash to the ground.

"You'll suffer for this. I'll cut your fucking hair off and hang it above his grave."

"What the hell happened to you?" I gasp, trying to fight her off as she waves the knife around. "You were supposed to be my friend."

"I was never your friend, you foolish, stupid girl. This was for him. It was all for him."

"It's funny you do so much for him, yet he never once mentioned you," I scream in her face.

She freezes for a second, and I know I've hit her hard.

It's enough of a hesitation.

I drive my fist up and into her face. The loud crunch her nose makes has my skin crawling, but it works. She rolls off me with a scream and I roll to my left, lunging for the knife. She goes for it too and manages to get it just before I do. I jerk backwards quickly and roll again, tucking in close. I push to my feet and spin around, wanting to get some distance between us before she has the chance to use it.

She's on her feet again. Blood runs down her face, her hair is wild, and her knees are swollen and bruised. She holds the knife in her hand, and her eyes are wild. This is the moment, I can feel it in my bones. This is the moment it'll end for one of us.

We both stare. Panting.

"You were my friend," I say, my voice thick. "I trusted you. You're nothing but an evil monster, and you will suffer the same fate as your pathetic, useless father. He couldn't beat me, and neither will you."

"Don't you talk about him like that," she yells hysterically.

She's losing it. So I continue. "It's the truth. Clayton was pathetic, and so are you. Your game is pathetic. You're both losers."

Her body jerks and her eyes flare.

"He'd be ashamed that not even you could finish it for him. His precious daughter. The one who was supposed to get justice. Yet look at you. You are lame."

She flinches again.

"Failures. Both of you."

She lunges. "I'll fucking end you, Marlie Jacobson. For Daddy. I'll end you."

As if in slow motion, her body comes hurtling towards me. I lunge backwards but don't realize there is a log behind me. Panic grips me as I start to fall, and her body comes towards mine. *Oh God. No.* Fear grips my chest as I flail, trying to stop myself from falling. Hannah has the knife poised, and she's wearing an incredible smile. A victory smile.

The second my back hits the ground, I'm dead.

I know it.

She knows it.

She's going to drive that knife into my body.

I hit the ground and clench my eyes shut the moment pain radiates through my spine from the hard ground beneath me. A loud gunshot rings out, piercing the still air. A body falls over mine, but the knife doesn't penetrate. The body is still.

Limp. My eyes fly open and Hannah is on top of me, unmoving. It takes me a moment to figure out what's happened.

She's not moving.

There is blood running from her chest onto mine.

Someone shot her.

Someone . . .

"Marlie!"

In a haze, I turn my head slowly, wondering if I'm imagining the voice.

"Marlie!"

Kenai?

My vision blurs.

Kenai appears from behind a row of trees. He rushes over, flipping Hannah off me before pulling me to my feet. My body sways. My knees tremble. I stare up at him.

He saved me.

Kanai saved my life.

I collapse against his chest, and his arms go around me.

"Oh fuck. Thank God you're okay, Marlie. Tell me you're okay."

"She's gone," I whisper against his chest, my vision swimming. "You saved me."

"I know. I know. It's okay. It's going to be okay."

"I . . . she's gone . . ."

"I know, baby. It's over. It's all over. You're safe now."

"It's over," I murmur into his chest.

"It's over."

"Kaity?"

"Safe. You saved her life."

I saved her life.

I saved them.

And he saved me.

Like I always knew he would.

THIRTY

"Where are they! Where are my daughters?"

My mother's frantic voice echoes from outside my hospital room, and I stir awake. My vision is hazy as I listen to Kenai's voice.

"They're okay, but right now they don't want them to have visitors. They've been continually questioned over the last day and they're tired. Let them rest. Come back later."

"They're my daughters, I need to see them."

"No," Kenai says, his voice firm. "What you need to do is go, leave them be, and sort your own shit out. I don't know you, ma'am, and I don't pretend to, but you nearly lost the two best things in your life yesterday. I can tell you something for nothing, no amount of money in the world can ever replace the gift you have in those girls."

"Who the hell are you?" Mom shrieks.

"I'm someone who cares about them. Go. And if you care about them, if you truly love them, get yourself together and realize what you've got before it's too late. Those girls need a mother. Not a money-hungry gold digger."

"How dare you! Those are my daughters."

"And what have you done for them?"

Silence.

"If you love them, even a little fucking bit, go away and come back only when you're ready to be a mother. To be there for them. To comfort them. To help them heal. That's what they need. They don't need reporters. Or books. Or money. They need you. And you're doing a terrible job at being what they need."

More silence.

"Do them a favor. Fix yourself."

"I just . . ." she begins. "I just wanted to see if they were okay."

"They're okay. But right now, they need to be left alone."

A nurse comes in, and I'm cut off from the conversation when she closes the door behind her. "Hi. You're awake?"

I nod, shifting uncomfortably. Both my hands are bandaged, and one is in a cast.

"How are you feeling?" she asks, starting her routine observations.

"Okay," I croak. "Where's my sister?"

"She's being treated."

"I need to see her. Please."

"I'll speak with a doctor."

She finishes up what she's doing and heads out just as Kenai walks in. "Hi," he murmurs.

My heart swells that he defended me, even though he has no idea that I heard it. I love him in that moment. More than anything in my entire world.

"Hi," I whisper.

He stops at my bed and looks down at me, running a thumb over my cheek. "You okay?"

"She's gone, Kenai," I say, my heart aching. "I know she was crazy, but once, she was my friend."

Kenai gently climbs into the bed and pulls me close, tucking me into him, right where I need to be. "You escaped another nightmare. Hannah was never your friend. Even if you tried to be hers. You were so brave, Marlie. You saved Kaitlyn and you saved Yasmin. Without you, they might be gone now."

"I never wanted her to die, though," I say softly.

"No, but sometimes you don't get to choose how these things end. I know it's hard, but you're so damned incredible and brave."

"It's really over?" I say, looking up at him. I love his face. I love everything about him. He stares down at me with a soft expression. His features gentle. Real.

"It's really over. You're safe."

My chest exhales with relief. *Safe*. A word I wondered if I could ever hear and truly believe, but I do. I believe in it now. Not just because

Clayton and Hannah are gone, but because I have Kenai. I know with my whole heart he'll never let anything happen to me again.

"I want to see Kaity."

He nods, tucking me closer. "Just let me hold you for a second more."

My heart swells and I nestle into him, feeling a comfort I haven't felt in such a long time. A warmth. Something so real and beautiful. "Were you afraid?"

He flinches. "So fucking afraid. I thought I was going to lose you. I'm sorry, Marlie. I should have listened to you."

"You mean instead of being a jerk?" I tease.

He laughs lightly. "Yeah, instead of being a jerk. You forgive me?"

"That depends?" I say, tilting my head back. "Are you going to be okay with my new haircut?"

He grins down at me, running his hand through my now short hair. Hannah made a mess of it when she tried to remove it, and they had to cut a bunch off to be able to treat the wound at the back of my head. They cut the rest so it didn't look uneven.

"You'd look beautiful no matter what."

"I think that's the nicest thing you've ever said to me. Anyone would think you like me."

He presses a kiss to my nose. "I do fucking like you, Marlie Jacobson. Damn, do I like you."

My heart swells.

He likes me.
Finally.

"I was so afraid," Kaity whispers, holding me close.

The doctors finally let us in together. It took a lot of convicing, but they said if we didn't exert ourselves, we could lie together for a while. I don't know what it is they think we're going to do in here. Run a marathon? Skip around the room? Honestly. Still, we managed to shuffle into the bed beside each other, and we haven't moved since.

"It's all over now," I say. "We're going to be okay."

"Yasmin, is she okay?" Kaity asks.

"Last I heard she got discharged after her fingers were set and they put some stitches in her arm. You saved her life, Kaity."

Kaity shakes her head. "No. You did. You got us out of there."

"I got you out the door, and the rest was on you. I'm so proud."

She snuggles closer. "It was terrifying, Marlie. Being in there, wondering if I was going to be okay, wondering if I was ever going to see the people I loved again, wondering if I was ever going to be free. I felt just a fraction of the fear you felt, and it was enough to nearly destroy me."

I hug her closer. "But it didn't destroy you. And it won't. Take it from me, letting it eat you alive is only going to halve your life. We escaped. We made it. We have the chance to do something good, something amazing."

"I've been thinking," Kaity says. "Maybe there is something we can do. Something to raise awareness, not just for people who have been in a situation like that, but for anyone who's scared or afraid. Being there, being alone and scared, it was the worst feeling in the world. But some people live like that every day, in all kinds of situations. I want to do something. I want some good to come out of this."

Pride swells in my chest. "You're incredible, Kaity. I think you're right. I think we should do something for those people out there who are afraid and alone."

She nods, and nestles in. "I heard Kenai yelling at Mom earlier."

"Yeah, he sent her away."

"Nobody has ever defended us like that before," she whispers. "I like him, Marlie."

"I like him too, honey."

"Will you do something for me?"

I nod. "Of course. Anything."

"Will you keep him?"

I laugh softly. "I will try."

"Marlie?"

"Mmmm?"

"Are you going to be okay?"

I know what she's asking. She's asking if I'm going to be okay after surviving yet another horror. I don't honestly know how to answer that question. After Clayton, I was so afraid, so broken, so horrified. But after surviving Hannah's attack—and seeing Kaity come through it so admirably—I feel stronger, more determined, like I might actually get through this one unscathed. I guess there are really only two choices for me. I can let it eat me alive, like last time, or I can use the experience to do some good, like Kaity plans to do.

Either way, it won't take away what happened.

It's up to me to choose how I live with it.

I look to Kaity and meet her eyes. "Yeah, I am going to be okay. It won't be easy. There will be times when it's hard. But I have you, and I have Kenai, and we're okay. Finally, we're okay. I won't let you down again, Kaity. I won't lose you once more. I won't sink. I think you're right. We have a chance to do something amazing."

She smiles and takes my hand.

"I know exactly what we should do," she says. "Do you trust me?"

I smile. "Always, little sister."

Always.

THIRTY-ONE

"Marlie, Kaitlyn, can you tell us why you decided to open this place?"

I tuck my hand into Kaity's and smile for the camera, knowing how hard this is on her. I remember how afraid I was when the press first aimed their cameras at me. I remember exactly how it felt. Sure, our situation is different, but it's still terrifying and it's still nice to know you have someone holding your hand, just in case you fall.

I decide to speak.

"We created a safe place for abuse victims, be they women, children, even men. A place where they can come to escape, to feel safe."

"What types of abuse?" a reporter asks, shoving a microphone towards my face.

"As you know, I've been in the hands of two killers, and one of them attacked my sister. It's safe to say I've learned a few things during those times." I pause for effect. "I know how it feels afterwards. I know how it feels to be alone. The abuse Kaitlyn and I suffered was just one type. There are hundreds of people out there who are living through some terrifying ordeals. We want them to know they have a place they could come to feel safe."

"What a wonderful idea," a reporter says, stepping up closer. "Kaitlyn, did you have input in this idea?"

All the cameras swing to Kaity, and for a moment I think she'll choke, but instead she lets my hand go, takes a deep breath, and steps forward. "The center was definitely something I had input in. I too wanted to provide a safe place for everyone who feels there is no escape, who live with fear consuming their lives daily. I never truly understood what my sister went through until my own ordeal, and if I can provide comfort to someone feeling the same thing, then I'm more than willing."

"When will the center open?" a reporter shouts.

"How will you fund it?" asks another.

"Will you work there?"

"Are you still seeing Kenai Michelson?"

"We are currently working on finding a location for the center, and will announce details shortly. Thank you," I say.

I turn to Kaity. "That's all we need to give them."

I take her hand again, and we push past the reporters.

Just before we get inside, a soft voice calls out. "Marlie? Kaity?"

We both turn to see Yasmin on the sidewalk, flowers in her hand, smiling at us. She looks radiant with her beautiful silvery white hair framing her beaming face. But mostly, she looks happy.

"Yasmin!" I say, stepping forward. "How are you?"

"I'm sorry to just barge in on you, but I heard you'd be here today and I wanted to see you both. Especially you, Marlie. I didn't get a chance to see you after we got to the hospital, but I want to thank you for what you did for me. Words can't express how grateful I am that you saved my life."

My heart swells and I step forward, pulling her in for a hug. She hesitates for a second, then gladly accepts. I hang on to her for a second, then Kaity joins in and we all hug, reporters be damned.

When we pull back, I ask her, "Are you okay? Are you doing well?"

She nods. "I've been getting help, and I feel like I'm healing. I'm getting there. I still have hard days, but mostly I'm just grateful I'm alive."

"I'm glad," I say, squeezing her arm.

"If you and Kaity are in town again soon, maybe we can catch up?" she suggests. "Here's my number."

She hands me a slip of paper.

"That would be awesome!" Kaity grins.

I nod, too.

"Okay." Yasmin smiles, her face lighting up.

"Well, give me a call. I should get going, my mom is waiting. Thank you both again."

"Talk soon." I wave.

"Bye!" Kaity calls as we head inside.

After a long day at the center, a sleek black truck pulls up to the curb, and we both climb in. The second I'm buckled up, I turn and smile at the love of my life. Kenai is dressed casually, hair messy, stubble on his chin. The same gorgeous, dominating man I fell in love with. The same one who risked it all to save my life. I don't know where I'd be without him.

"Hi there." I smile, reaching over and taking his hand.

"Was that Yasmin I just saw?"

"Yeah, she wanted to say thanks and see if we wanted to catch up soon."

He grins. "Must have been good to see her."

"Yeah, it really was. I've been wondering how she's been doing."

"It makes you feel good, too," Kaity pipes up from the back seat. "Knowing she's okay, knowing we all are."

"Yeah," I say, shuffling deeper into the seat with a big smile on my face. "Yeah, it really does."

"Proud of you, beautiful," Kenai says, giving me a soft expression. An expression I'm learning to love more and more, because he saves it just for me.

I smile and look out the window. "You know,

Kenai, I think Kaity and I might just change the world."

Kaity giggles from the back seat.

Kenai squeezes my hand. "I could have told you that."

I smile.

Kaity laughs.

Kenai is right beside me.

All is right in the world again.

A few months later and here I am about to cut the ribbon to the place I've been working so hard to open. Hundreds of people are gathered out in front of Sanctuary, waiting for it to open. Most of them just want to meet Kaity and me. But also in the crowd I can see the faces: the faces of the terrified, the worn, the tired, the scared, the lonely. They're amongst them, shrinking away from the crowd yet waiting, with hope in their eyes, for a place where they can feel safe.

"I now declare Sanctuary open," Kaity yells as the red ribbons falls.

The crowd cheers as Kenai steps up beside me, talking into his cell phone. He says something, then hangs up and puts an arm around Kaity and me. "Are you girls ready for this?"

We both nod, take a deep breath, and step to the side. The crowd rushes in, all them wanting to see what we've done to the inside. What kinds of services we provide. This is a massive moment. The opening of Sanctuary is everything. It will be in every newspaper and news story in the city, so we needed to make sure that when people stepped inside it for the first time, they felt it, they truly felt it.

I take a shaky breath, and then we all enter.

I stop as I step in to look around. Putting myself back in their shoes, letting my fear rise up and letting my body have a natural reaction to the space around me. I look at it through fresh eyes, and I really take it in.

This incredible place.

The space is huge, open and filled with such beauty it takes my breath away. We made it warm, lining the floors with sandy-colored wood planks. We kept the lights bright but warm, the walls a soft cream. The left wall, from one end to the other and top to bottom, is lined with books. All of them donated by people around the world wanting to help our cause—something Kenai set up. There are ladders that slide across the shelves, so people can climb up to get a book, and back down to spend hours browsing.

In the space are massive lounges and coffee stations, plush and warm, with throw pillows and blankets. Right in the middle is a large fireplace. A zone for people to feel safe and warm and content. A place where they can forget their troubles, a place where their fears are left behind. The building is fully secured and guarded. We want them to know that when they come in here, the ugly of the world can't touch them.

Moving on from the library section, I glance over at the massive kitchen lining the back wall. Stocked with everything. I've hired cooks to make food daily—comfort food, food for the soul, food that make people feel safe and at home. In front of the kitchen is a station set up for sewing, knitting, arts and crafts, and painting. My therapist told me these things are good for distraction and mind processing. She said it would be an important station to have.

On the right side of the room are television screens, with hundreds of available movies, in front of big, comfy lounges. We purchased a massive popcorn machine and a soda machine that we will keep constantly stocked. All the movies are fun, romantic, and carefully picked with the help of experts to ensure good feelings.

And in the middle of the space is a massive circle of lounges, with coffee tables in the center. A place where people can sit and talk about the world, where they can make friends, meet like-minded people, or just sit and listen to others talk. A place where they can express their thoughts, or write, or sleep if that's what they need to do.

I press a hand to my heart and a tear rolls down my cheek.

"You did incredible, sweetheart," Kenai says, stepping up beside me, curling a hand around my waist and pulling me close. "This is all you."

"Kaitlyn too. I knew I had to change something, but she insisted that we needed to use our experiences for something good. I just never thought it would be this . . . this . . ."

"Fucking incredible?"

I turn to him and press my face into his chest as my nose tingles from emotion.

"I'm proud of you, Marlie. So fucking proud. You make the world a better place. You're giving people an escape. You're providing a safe place. That takes guts, it takes determination, but mostly it takes an incredibly big heart. Look around you, and love what you've done. The lives that will be saved because of this place . . . I don't think you'll ever fully grasp."

I sob and clutch him tighter.

Someone comes up behind us and wraps their arms around me.

Kaity.

She hangs on to me, resting her head on my back. "We did this," she whispers.

I let Kenai go and turn to face my sister. She had to clip all of her beautiful red hair off. It's now styled in a pixie cut, which suits her. She's always been beautiful, but now more than ever. She has the same light in her eyes. The same hope. The same determination to help others. She didn't let our experience beat her, she let it define her and create who she is.

"We did this, but mostly, you did this," I whisper back.

"I love you, Marlie," she says, hugging me tight.

"I love you, too."

"Girls."

Kaity and I both look to see our mother standing there with a bunch of flowers in her hands. We haven't seen a lot of her since the ordeal with Hannah, both of us too disappointed in her behavior to make any further effort to contact her. So seeing her here . . . it's shocking. She hasn't reached out to us for months, and we both figured she'd just moved on with her life without us. She looks nervous, but her eyes widen as she takes it all in.

"I know there is nothing I can possibly say that will ever change what I did to you both," she says as she looks to me then to Kaity.

"I don't know why you're here," Kaity says, her voice shaky.

Mom reaches into her purse and pulls out a check. She hands it to me, and with trembling hands I take it.

"I failed as a mother. I know that now. The way I treated you after what happened, the way I let Kaity slip, the way I surrounded myself with that money. I was wrong. I have problems. I'm getting help to try and work on them. That can't make up for what I've lost because of my actions, but I hope this can help you two create the life you both deserve. This place, it's incredible. I'm so proud of my daughters."

Tears burn under my eyelids and Kaity reaches over, grabbing my hand.

"I sold the house," she says. "That's everything

I got from it. I want you to use it for your foundation, or for whatever you'd like. It's up to you. I've got a job and a little apartment in town. I'm doing well. It was never my money. It was always yours, Marlie. But the fact of the matter is, I should have never released that book. I should have been a mother when you needed me, and I wasn't. I can't take that back, but I can try and make it better now. I hope it helps you both change the world with this place. Because you're doing an incredible thing and I couldn't be happier for you both."

Kaity looks to me, and I look to her. It's the kindest thing our mother has ever done in her life—for anyone. She made an effort. She's trying. It's more than we could have ever expected or asked for. So, I do the only thing that seems right after everything I've been through. I step forward and hug her. She trembles, and then bursts out crying when Kaity steps in and hugs her too.

"We still have a very long way to go before this can ever be okay again," I say to her, when we step back. "But thank you so much for doing this."

She nods, swiping her eyes. "I hope we can see each other again soon. I've missed you both."

Kaity and I both nod, and Mom hands her the flowers.

"We'll talk soon," I promise her.

She nods, smiles, and looks around, and then she's gone.

I turn to Kaity. "You okay?"

She nods, smiling. "Yeah, I think I'm going to be just fine."

I grin. "Me too."

She steps back, smiles at Kenai, and disappears into the crowd. Kenai takes my hand and leads me out the back door to the little courtyard we created for the staff to be able to take breaks. He turns to me and cups my face in his hands. " "You okay?"

I nod. "I never thought I'd see the day she'd do that, but the fact that she did means she deserves a second chance. Even if it'll take a while for us to trust her again. That was on you."

He gives me a confused look and I smile. "Kaity and I heard what you said to her in the hospital that day, Kenai. You defended us. You put her in her place. If you didn't do that, she might have never changed. Thank you."

He grins. "Eavesdropping is rude, baby."

I giggle. "I never claimed to be polite."

He smiles. "Words will never describe the pride and admiration I feel when I look at you. To come out the other side of an ordeal like that—twice—stronger and better. So many people can say they have that strength, but you do. You have it and you made the most out of it."

"I couldn't have done it without you," I say, pressing my lips against his.

"You could have, because you, Marlie Jacobson, are the most incredible woman I've ever met in my entire life. You're beautiful and brave, but mostly you're strong and determined. I'm glad you came into my office that day."

"Are you?" I grin, cupping his chin and stroking my thumb over his jaw.

"Well, you were a little bossy and a bit crazy—"

I smack his chest.

He chuckles and pulls me closer. "I love you, my little warrior."

"And I love you, Chief."

He grunts.

I smile.

Then we both turn and stare at the building in front of us.

"I did this," I whisper.

"Yeah, baby, you did this."

"He didn't win."

Kenai wraps an arm around me, squeezing me close. "Neither did she."

"Turns out you can beat the monsters."

"Always."

Another tear rolls down my cheek as I stare up at a place I hope can create a comfort bubble for those in need. A place that will provide comfort when they're alone, and safety when they're scared. A place they can consider home.

It's home to me.

It's home to Kaity.

Now, it's going to be home to thousands more.

EPILOGUE

SIX MONTHS LATER

My eyelids flutter open, and it takes me a moment to realize there is sunlight pouring in and warming my face. I blink once, then twice, then look over beside me to where Kenai is sleeping, his breathing soft, his big arms wrapped around me, his face peaceful. Something warm swells in my chest, something real and true. I shuffle closer to him, needing to feel his warmth, needing to feel his comfort, but mostly needing him.

I'll always need him.

Especially right now.

"Kenai," I whisper.

He stirs, but doesn't wake.

I roll in his arms and kiss his shoulder. "Kenai, honey, wake up."

He stirs again, and with a yawn his eyes flutter open. He turns to me, pinning me with those gorgeous eyes. "What is it?" he asks, his voice husky from sleep.

"It happened."

He shakes his head in confusion. "What happened?"

"You said it would, but I didn't believe you. But . . . it happened."

"Not following you, baby."

"What time is it?"

He shrugs. "Morning."

"Kenai . . . it's morning."

He shakes his head, still confused.

"It's morning, and how did you sleep?"

It registers, and a huge smile breaks out over his face. "I slept the whole night through, and . . . so did you."

"So did I," I whisper, smiling. "I slept the entire night through, without waking once."

"No nightmares."

"You said it would happen, that one day I'd wake up without them, and you were right. I did. For the first time, I woke up without them."

He smiles, big and beautiful. "How does it feel?"

I snuggle in closer. "I could have them every night from now on, but I'll always remember how it felt to wake up this morning and feel peace for the first time in forever. Even if one day is all I get, it'll be enough."

He strokes a piece of hair from my forehead and leans closer, kissing my nose. "There are going to be plenty more mornings where I get to wake up and see your beautiful, carefree smile. I'll make sure of it."

"Then I'll spend the rest of my days a happy girl."

He winks at me. "You're already lucky enough. I mean, look at who is lying in bed next to you."

I giggle and kiss him.

"Don't get too cocky, Chief. I wouldn't want you to stop fighting to impress me."

He deepens the kiss, tangling his fingers in my hair.

"I'll never stop fighting for you, Marlie Jacobson. Even when you're driving me crazy, I'll still be fighting."

God.

This man.

Perfect.

"She's been sitting over there for an hour," Kaity says, pointing to the gorgeous blonde sitting on one of our plush sofas, just staring at her hands. She looks like she needs to talk, but like most people that come into Sanctuary, she doesn't know who to approach or where to start. That's what we're here for, to get the ball rolling.

"I'll take this one," I say, squeezing Kaity's hand and walking towards the woman.

She looks up as I approach, and her blue eyes find mine. She looks terrified, but otherwise well. She's got bright eyes, soft blonde hair, healthy skin. I sit down beside her and in a soft voice I've learned to master over the last few months, I ask her, "Are you okay?"

"You're Marlie, right?"

"Yes."

"I've heard about this place," she says, rubbing her hands together, "but I didn't know if I should come in here. I'm not an abuse survivor or anything, in fact nobody has ever hurt me but . . ."

"There are no rules on who can come in here," I say carefully. "Everyone is welcome. I can see something is wrong. Do you want to tell me what it is?"

"My sister . . . she's . . . missing."

My heart aches, because I know how that feels. I know it better than anyone.

"I'm so sorry. How can I help?"

"I know your sister went missing, I know she was taken by a killer . . . I . . . I think mine has been, too."

My skin prickles. I know Clayton and Hannah weren't the only killers out there in the world, but hearing the same fears in another person, knowing that there are still so many bad people out there, makes my heart ache. I can help only so many people, though I'd love to help them all.

"What makes you say that?"

"You've heard of the killings happening in and around Denver on television, right? The ones where the killer is studying women, then tormenting them with their worst fears, then taking and killing them, before stringing them up in a tree with a bowtie around their necks?"

I shiver. I have seen that on the news. They've found two victims so far. But no suspect.

"Yes, I have heard of that. You think your sister has been taken by this person?"

"Yes. But the police won't believe me because she never reported anything odd. But she told me, she told me strange things had been happening. She told me she had met a man and he was seemingly normal . . . but then she disappeared. She just . . . vanished. There was a note in her handwriting, left behind, saying she just needed time away. The police said as far as they can tell, she made a choice to leave. They're wrong. I know he has her."

"I believe you," I say, reaching out and squeezing her hand. "I'm going to help you out. I don't do this often, but for you I will, because I know how it feels to have nobody believe you. My boyfriend is the best tracker around. I'm going to call in a favor and see if he can help you."

"You will?"

I smile at her. "Of course. He helped me with my sister. He's the best at his job."

"Thank you so much," she whispers. "I'm just so afraid."

I squeeze her hand again. "Have faith, stay strong, and never, never stop fighting. Fight to make people believe you, fight for your sister, just keep fighting."

"Keep fighting," she says, nodding her head. "Thank you, Marlie."

"That's what we're here for."

I get her contact information and promise her Kenai will call her. I watch her disappear through the front doors then pull out my phone to dial Kenai.

"Hi, beautiful," he answers on the second ring.

"Hi there," I say. "Listen, I have a huge favor."

"Does it involve you and me getting naked?"

I laugh. "Animal. No. I had a girl come in here today, she thinks her sister has been taken by a killer. The police don't believe her. I told her you'd help out. You know I never do this, I never call in favors because you're so busy and—"

"I'll do it," he says.

I blink. "You will?"

"Yeah, I will. I will because you don't ask anything of me, you deal with everyone who comes into that place on your own, so if you're asking, I know it's important to you."

"God," I say, softly. "Have I told you how much I love you today?"

"You have, but feel free to tell me again."

I laugh. "I love you, Chief."

"Love you too, baby. I wouldn't take on another killer case if I didn't."

I shiver. "Another killer tormenting people. When will it stop?"

"It won't," he says, his voice soft. "But we'll all keep on fighting to make it less and less."

"I hope her sister is okay."

"Me too." He sighs. "Me too."

I say my goodbyes and hang up the phone, then I google the recent killings and read over the details.

Does this person truly have her sister?

And if so, is it too late?

I press my phone to my chest and send out a prayer.

I might be only one person, but one person can indeed change the world.

I can't fix everything.

I can't save everyone.

But I'll give it a damned good go.

It's my purpose. It's my mission.

And now, it's my passion.

Read on for an excerpt from
Bella Jewel's next book

BLIND DATE

Available in August 2017 from
St. Martin's Paperbacks

PROLOGUE

"I miss you, Ray." I see her lips mouth a touching tribute to her husband as she places a bright bunch of flowers by the headstone.

My eyes zone in on her—small, but strong, kneeling near a puddle of water as she runs her fingers over her husband's headstone. Her mousy brown hair is tucked neatly at the nape of her neck, pinned with a black clip. I wonder if she did that herself? Maybe her friend did, the one standing to her left, staring down at her with a soft look on her face.

My heart flickers.

But it isn't out of pity for the girl. No, it's pure joy. She's unlike anything I've ever seen before, unlike anything I've ever had experience with. I've been watching her for a while. All the rest—their situations were different. But this one . . . she's strong-willed. I can see it in the way she clenches her fists, stopping herself from breaking down. She isn't the kind to fall to her knees and scream. She's stronger than that. It's written all over her, right down to the hard set of her jaw as she holds herself back from crying.

No. She's not like the weak-willed women I've played with in the past.

I can feel it in my chest—she is the one. She's the goal. The ultimate prize. I can't rush with her. No, I have to take this slow; break her into tiny little pieces before I attack. I need to do my research and get this right. She isn't going to be easy, but she's going to be worth it. She is going to be the one I remember forever; I can feel it right down into my bones.

Yes. She's what I've practiced so hard for.

I'll have to change up my game. I can't do this the way I've done it with all the other women. This one is special and deserves special treatment. She's going to get everything that I've got bottled up inside for all this time. I'm going to play this one differently and make this girl my trophy. I'm going to swoop into her life like a hurricane, only she won't be able to see me; she'll feel me, though. I'll be back for her.

She'll never know what hit her.

Hartley Watson.

I'm coming for you.

CHAPTER ONE

"C'mon, Hart, it's been four years. You can't keep hiding away, avoiding the world."

I glance at Taylor, my best friend and a royal pain in my ass, and grimace. "Maybe so, but going on a blind date hardly seems like the ideal situation to get back out there. I've read about those, they never end well."

Taylor raises a pretty blond brow; even giving me a sarcastic expression she looks gorgeous. Blond, tall, lean, and fit. She doesn't need to worry about finding a date—she has them lining up. "How would you know? You've never been on one. You were with Raymond for ten years. When was the last time you even knew what it was like to meet a new person?"

The mention of my husband's name has my chest constricting. It's not as bad as it used to be. During those first few years after I lost him in a car accident, there was a stabbing pain every living, breathing moment. I don't think I went a day without that pain cutting through me. But over time, it turned into a slow ache, some days worse, some days barely there, but always a constant, in one way or another. A continuous reminder that he's gone, and that I'm still here without him. At least I can wake up without tears running down my cheeks now. That was a big step.

That was when I first felt like I was finally healing. It was six months ago.

"I don't want to meet any new people." I shrug. "Not by forcing it, anyway. It seems wrong . . ."

Taylor keeps that eyebrow raised, and crosses her arms, causing the purple blouse she's wearing to crumple up at the front. "Look, honey, I know you might not want to be ready, or even want to think about it, but it can't hurt to go on a date. It's not like you have to marry the guy. You have a few drinks and if you don't like him, you leave and never have to see him again."

I study her for a moment. She's stubborn. She doesn't budge when she gets an idea in her head. Those hazel eyes hold mine without hesitation, without even flickering in a different direction. She won't back down, and I damn well know it. When Taylor is in one of her "life-changing" moods, nobody can tell her no. Nobody.

"You're not going to let this go, are you?" I mumble, turning my attention away and squinting as I try to feed a piece of cotton into a needle so I can sew a button onto my favorite green blouse that I've probably far outworn, but I can't part with it. It's comfortable, so incredibly comfortable. And it was the last thing I wore when Raymond was alive. The last thing he touched. The last thing he saw me in.

Taylor makes a little sound in her throat, bringing my full attention back. "Hart, you're young and you could be out there, getting all the love you deserve. Can you just do this for me? Please? Go on a few dates, and if you hate them I swear I'll never ever mention it again. I'll leave you to sew buttons and stay huddled up in this apartment for another four years, wasting away."

I give her a foul look and she blinks innocently at me.

Damn her. She's good. She knows how to push my buttons and get beneath the surface to stir me up and get what she wants. We've known each other too long, that's the problem. She might as well be my sister, my other half, basically a part of me. And she can read me like a damned book.

"One," I say, looking back down and feeding the needle through the button and then through the material of my blouse. "One date, and that's it."

"Five."

I snort. "One."

"Four dates. C'mon, Hartley."

She puts her hands together in a pleading gesture. Those big eyelashes batting as she looks at me, like some sort of desperate kitten.

I narrow my eyes at her. "Two."

"Three and we'll call it even."

I sigh. "I don't know why I have to go out with three men. Can't I just go out on one date and be done with it? I'm not interested in seeing anyone. I'm not sure I'll ever be interested in dating anyone again. Honestly."

She's already smiling way too big, because she knows she's won. She knows it and she's thrilled with it. "You don't know until you try, and hey, you might even just find a friend out of it. Wouldn't it be nice to have a friend at the very least?"

I squint at her again. "Last time I checked, that's what you are."

She smiles prettily. "Yes, but I mean a male friend. One who might make you laugh. Who might make you feel good again."

"You do all of that," I mumble, putting the needle between my lips as I try to adjust the button. I know what she means but I'm not going to give her the satisfaction of admitting it.

"Stop arguing with me, and just do as you're told."

I giggle and the needle drops from my lips. I know what she's doing, and I know it's probably time I give in and start getting back out there, but the very idea of dressing up and going on a date makes me cringe. I don't think it's because I don't want to, I mean, sure, one day I do want to meet someone. I guess it's just the fear of being that . . . open with someone again.

I never really dated Ray. We met through mutual friends when we were in our early twenties and we just sort of started talking—he made me laugh, I'll always remember that. During our first conversation, he had me in hysterics. One thing led to another and before I knew it, we were together. Sure, we went out after that, but there was never the awkward first date moment, where the possibility of getting stuck with a stranger for at least an hour is high.

Then there is the issue of trying to figure out something to say. I groan inwardly, I'm honestly not sure I'm cut out for this. I've never been good with new people, let alone small talk, but Taylor is right, it has been four years and I've held myself back. I can't do that forever. So maybe enduring a few dates is, at the very least, a step in the right direction. I don't want to be alone forever, I truly don't, but I won't deny that the idea of stepping back into the terrifying world of dating does frighten me a little.

"Fine," I give in, and sigh. "Three, but that's it. When it doesn't work out with any of them, and it likely won't, then you leave me alone and mention nothing of the male species again."

She claps her hands together. "It's a deal, but you have to at least try. I don't want to hear you showed up on your worst behavior and ruined things before the men even got to say a word."

I huff. "You just ruined my plan. I was going to wear my ugliest jeans, and dribble while I ate."

She slaps my arm and I grin up at her.

"Don't be smart, Hartley. Trust me, this is going to be good for you."

I grunt. It'll definitely be something for me, but whether good is the word I'd use is to be determined. "Where, dare I ask, are you going to find these three eligible bachelors?"

She grins mischievously and rubs her hands together. I don't want to hear her answer, not when she's giving me a look that screams she's been up to no good. "I've already found them."

She. *Wait . . . what?* How in the hell could she have found three men, in such a short time?

"Taylor!"

She puts her hands up in self-defense as I throw the nearest item at her, which happens to be a roll of thread. It bounces off her shoulder and trails across the floor, leaving a long line of string in its path. Great. That'll take forever to roll back up.

"Come on, you didn't think I would get you to agree without having this all ready to go, did you?"

I scowl at her. That's exactly what I was thinking. I

figured I had at least a few weeks or maybe she'd move on to something else and forget about it entirely. Besides, where in the hell does she have time to find three men for me, as well as work, and basically attempt to run my entire life?

She rolls her eyes. "Stop scowling, Hart, you need to start using that beautiful smile to attract these gorgeous prospects."

I roll my eyes right back. "Where did you find three men?"

"I found five, actually, but I can narrow it down to three. And there is this singles website, it's actually called **blind date**. It's really super cool. You put in all your details, what you're looking for, right down to the way someone looks, and it sends you matches. You ask them for a date, they agree or disagree. If they agree, you set up a location and meet. It's kind of mysterious, don't you think?"

I wouldn't go as far as saying mysterious. I can count at least ten ways that could go wrong. I mean, seriously, it's like a website created for all the crazies of the world to lie and meet on dates. I don't know how the creator thought it would be a successful idea. Although, obviously it is successful because Taylor has found me not one, not two, but five men. Thank God I only agreed to three. "If I get sold as a sex slave, it's all your fault," I say, wiggling my finger at her.

She laughs. "Don't be so dramatic. You're far too mouthy for that. They'd sooner chop you into a thousand pieces before using you as a slave, you'd drive them crazy in a day."

I flip her the bird and she winks at me.

"The first date is tonight, by the way. I have a dress for you."

My eyes pop wide open. She's kidding? Tonight? My heart clenches in a strange way, nerves, maybe? It's been so long since I've felt anything even remotely like the anxious feeling bubbling in my tummy. Am I truly ready for this? I guess I'm not getting much of a choice. "Taylor, seriously . . ."

"You're welcome."

I pout at her. "There will be revenge for this. Sweet, sweet revenge."